PROTECTING OLYMPIA (SPECIAL FORCES: OPERATION ALPHA)

SEARCH & RESCUE BOOK 3

JEN TALTY

Dear Readers,

Welcome to the Special Forces: Operation Alpha Fan-Fiction world!

If you are new to this amazing world, in a nutshell the author wrote a story using one or more of my characters in it. Sometimes that character has a major role in the story, and other times they are only mentioned briefly. This is perfectly legal and allowable because they are going through Aces Press to publish the story.

This book is entirely the work of the author who wrote it. While I might have assisted with brainstorming and other ideas about which of my characters to use, I didn't have any part in the process or writing or editing the story.

I'm proud and excited that so many authors loved my characters enough that they wanted to write them into their own story. Thank you for supporting them, and me!

READ ON!

Xoxo

Susan Stoker

PRAISE FOR JEN TALTY

"*Deadly Secrets* is the best of romance and suspense in one hot read!" *NYT Bestselling Author Jennifer Probst*

"A charming setting and a steamy couple heat up the pages in a suspenseful story I couldn't put down!" *NY Times and USA today Bestselling Author Donna Grant*

"Jen Talty's books will grab your attention and pull you into a world of relatable characters, strong personalities, humor, and believable storylines. You'll laugh, you'll cry, and you'll rush to get the next book she releases!" Natalie Ann USA Today Bestselling Author

"I positively loved *In Two Weeks*, and highly recommend it. The writing is wonderful, the story is fantastic, and the characters will keep you coming back for more. I can't wait to get my hands on future installments of the NYS Troopers series." *Long and Short Reviews*

"*In Two Weeks* hooks the reader from page one. This is a fast paced story where the development of the romance grabs you emotionally and the suspense keeps you sitting on the edge of your chair. Great characters, great writing, and a believable plot that can be a warning to all of us." *Desiree Holt, USA Today Bestseller*

"*Dark Water* delivers an engaging portrait of wounded hearts as the memorable characters take you on a healing journey of love. A mysterious death brings danger and intrigue into the drama, while sultry passions brew into a believable plot that melts the reader's heart. Jen Talty pens an entertaining romance that grips the heart as the colorful and dangerous story unfolds into a chilling ending." *Night Owl Reviews*

"This is not the typical love story, nor is it the typical mystery. The characters are well rounded and interesting." *You Gotta Read Reviews*

"*Murder in Paradise Bay* is a fast-paced romantic thriller with plenty of twists and turns to keep you guessing until the end. You won't want to miss this one..." *USA Today bestselling author Janice Maynard*

To Amy. Your friendship and support means the world.

You rock sister!

CHAPTER 1

Olympia Anderson reached out and pressed her finger against the doorbell. She'd overheard her neighbor talking on the phone while he stood out on his balcony that he'd be heading down to the Sans Bar and Grill tonight. She'd been staking out Landon Asher for two weeks now, and it was high time she put her plan into motion.

The front door rattled open. "You're my new neighbor, right?" Landon Asher stood in front of her wearing only his jeans. He smelled of fresh mint and pine. His smoldering gaze tore through her body. Handsome didn't come close to describing Landon.

But it didn't matter.

He was a sailor and a liar.

"That's me," she said.

"I'm Landon." He arched a brow. "Does *that's me* have a name?"

Her pulse pounded against her temple. She had no idea if Landon would know who she was or not. Olympia wasn't considered your everyday run of the mill name and while her brother tended to keep to himself, she would expect her name would come up in conversation. She took in a quick breath. "Olympia," she said.

"That's an interesting name."

"So is Landon."

"It was my mother's maiden name, and since she had no brothers to carry on the name, she and my dad thought this was the next best thing."

She hadn't expected a dissertation in child naming, but it did make her feel more relaxed about the fact Landon didn't have a clue as to who she was. That had to be a good thing. "That's sweet."

"So, where'd your name come from?"

Holy crow. Was he going to stand there without a shirt, sucking on a beer, and flirt with her? Might be worth being friendly. "My mom's from Greece, and she just always loved the name."

"Makes sense. Now, what can I help you with?" Tall, dark, and sexy with the proverbial five o'clock shadow raised a glass bottle and brought it to his lips, taking a long draw.

"This is so embarrassing." She let out a long breath and crinkled her nose, doing her best to act as if she were totally mortified, which she sort of was, but this seemed like a more reasonable request than to ask for a cup of milk, sugar, or an egg. "Do you have a toilet plunger?"

"I do." He chuckled, stepping aside. "Come on in, and I'll go get it." He held open the door, making her duck under his arm.

He had to be at least six foot three and stuffed with lean muscles coated with a thin layer of bronzed skin that reminded her of a candy coating. He wasn't a body builder, but every inch of the man was defined by perfection. If she were any other woman, at any other time, and he wasn't in the military, she might entertain the idea.

"Do you need help with the toilet as well?" He set his beer on the kitchen counter. "I've got a few minutes, and I don't mind."

"I think I can handle it."

His condo was the exact same setup as hers, but she was surprised at the decor. Not so much that he had it filled with furniture, but that they matched, and he had a style that screamed modern beach with the white leather recliners and light-green sofa in the family room. He had a big picture of a turtle hanging over the couch and the opposing wall had a white-washed entertainment unit with beach and boating knickknacks on the shelves and a big screen television in the center.

His kitchen cabinets were light-gray shaker, just like hers, and the white-and-gray granite countertop was identical as well, but his floor was this wood-looking high-end vinyl that had a gray finish to it.

Damn, she had apartment envy. Perhaps he owned his. Wasn't unheard of for a single sailor to own his own place. But not usually the hot young ones.

Focus.

"I'll be right back." He turned and jogged up the stairs.

Good. That gave her a little more time to unlock a window. The question was which one. She did a quick scan and decided she'd do two things. First one would be to unlock the sliders. After she did that, then she made sure the window over the kitchen sink wasn't secure. Trying to act nonchalant, she leaned against the kitchen counter.

Landon came down the stairs, this time wearing a black T-shirt and a pair of boat shoes. "I'm heading out. You can either leave this on the back patio when you're done, or just return it tomorrow. But not until after ten, please. We're celebrating my buddy's recent elopement along with the fact his wife is expecting twins in a couple of months. They actually own the Sans down the street."

"Oh. Clover. The singer, right?" Olympia had gone into the local watering hole twice and had the pleasure of hearing Clover firsthand. Beautiful voice and gorgeous woman.

"That's right," Landon said. "Hey, would you like to come? I can wait a few minutes."

"No. I've got some things to do, but thank you."

"Offer stands if you change your mind. It's a private party, but I'll put your name on the guest list as my plus one."

Wow. He was casual and forward at the same time. Maybe if she didn't find anything that could help her, she'd try a different tactic. She followed him out the door and across the patio to her apartment.

He handed her the pail and plunger. "Are you sure you don't need help?"

"I can manage. It's not that bad."

"Suit yourself. Take care."

Standing on her stoop, she watched him stroll

down the sidewalk. The Sans was only a half mile down the street, so she wasn't surprised he chose to walk, but she'd wished he'd taken his Harley. That way she'd hear him coming a mile away and she'd be able to sneak out quickly.

Of course, she should also have a couple of hours to search his place. Since Woodrow worked in the administrative office for the SEAL teams stationed at the Joint Expeditionary Base - Little Creek in Virginia, she had no idea how much Landon crossed paths with her brother. The only thing she knew for sure was that Landon had been in the office the last time she spoke to her brother, and she knew that because her brother had called Landon by his name.

A few days later, her brother had gone AWOL.

As soon as Landon disappeared into the dark night, she raced back over to his place and slipped in through the sliders. That was easy. She let out a long breath, holding her cell up with a dim light. She wasn't exactly sure what she was looking for, but she'd know when she found it.

She started in the family room, opening the end table drawers but finding nothing other than blank pads of paper, a few decks of cards, and a game she'd never heard of. She made her way to the first-floor bedroom, which was also surprisingly nicely decorated for a bachelor with a teal picket fence headboard, matching nightstands, and white desk with a filing cabinet tucked underneath. Pulling out the office-style chair, she opened the top drawer and thumbed through the files, half hoping she'd find one labeled Woodrow Anderson.

When she found out her brother had gone missing, the Navy had treated it as if he'd gone AWOL, simply because he hadn't shown up for duty. But her brother loved the military. It was all he'd ever wanted to be, and he was happy to serve his country. Her brother wouldn't just disappear without telling her, especially when he'd been so upset.

She pulled out the second drawer and found nothing of interest. She should have known. Landon wasn't an investigator. Why would he be keeping files on people?

Maybe they were on his laptop.

She flipped it open, and it immediately asked for a password or thumbprint.

Shit.

As if she knew anything about him in order to make an educated guess as to what his password would be.

The light overhead flicked on.

She gasped, jerking in the chair.

"I think you're in the wrong condo." Landon casually leaned against the doorjamb with a gun in one hand, though thankfully pointed at the floor. "You have exactly two minutes to give me a good reason why I shouldn't call the police."

"Woodrow Anderson," she said with a frog-sized lump lodged in her throat. "You remember him?"

Landon arched a brow. "I do. Why?"

"He's my brother, and I think you know what happened to him." Her heart hammered in her chest. She wouldn't make a good criminal.

"Why would I know that?" Landon tucked his weapon into his pants.

"You were in the office the last time I spoke with my brother. He was agitated over something that happened." She needed to get Landon to see that all she wanted was information about her brother. That she was just trying to make sense of his disappearance.

"That doesn't mean I know why he went AWOL."

"That's the problem. Woodrow wouldn't just leave the Navy. He also wouldn't disappear without telling me. We're very close."

Landon stepped to the side, holding open the door. "If you wanted to ask me a question about your brother, you could have just done exactly that instead of breaking into my apartment. Now, I'd appreciate it if you'd leave. I need to get back to my party." He waved his hand in front of him. "I won't call the police. But if you do this again, I will."

As gracefully as she could, she stood, smoothing down the front of her pants. "What can you tell me about my brother? I know the Navy isn't telling me the truth."

Landon slowly blinked his eyes, shaking his head. "I barely knew Woodrow, and I have no idea what happened. You want to talk to Quinn Thatcher. She's the naval investigator who is looking into your brother's disappearance."

"I'm well aware of who she is, and she basically told me my brother is a fugitive, but I know something bad happened. I just know, and I can't get anyone to listen." She tapped her chest, fighting back the tears. Her twin brother was her entire world. He had the kind of spirit and sweet soul that made everyone else around him smile.

The Navy was his world. When he finished boot camp, he had told her that he'd finally found the place where he belonged.

"Until your brother is found, he's absolutely a wanted man," Landon said. "You don't get to just walk away from the military." He nodded his head toward the hallway. "Now it's time for you to leave."

"He didn't walk away. Something happened to him." She scooted past him, keeping her head down until she nearly ran right into an older gentleman. Not too old, but older than Landon. "Oh. Sorry," she mumbled.

"Might want to watch where you're going," the man said.

Landon chuckled. "Abe, meet my neighbor, Olympia."

"Nice to meet you, I think."

"You too," she said, tucking her hair behind her ears. She needed to get out of this apartment, and fast. In a day or two, she'd find a way to apologize to Landon and start over, because no way would she give up, and Landon was her only hope right now.

"Do you need an escort home?" Abe asked. "Or maybe to the nearest police station?"

She narrowed her eyes. "I can manage."

"Don't mind Abe. He gets a little big brotherish with me sometimes. I grew up down the street from him, and as you can tell, he's a *much* older than me."

"Why do you find that necessary to point out?" Abe said, shaking his head. "And I still think you should call the cops."

"Of course you do," Landon said, flattening his hand on her back. "We call him *Honest Abe* because he demands nothing less than the absolute truth. He's why I joined the Navy and became a SEAL, and before you ask, he met your brother once too."

"Who's her bro?"

"The kid who went AWOL last month."

"Woodrow?" Abe asked.

Her heart jumped into her throat. "You know my brother?"

"I wouldn't say that," Abe said. "But I've had some special assignments here, and Woodrow is always the one who deals with the paperwork. Nice young man. I'm sorry he's missing."

"Thank you." Tears stung the corners of her eyes.

"But you shouldn't go breaking into people's condos. Especially ones like Landon. He's got a small arsenal in here, and for someone who isn't a sniper, he's a damn good shot."

"I'll keep that in mind," she mumbled, making a beeline for the door.

"Don't forget to return my plunger," Landon said. "And you're still welcome to come to the party."

She raced across his patio and to hers, fumbling with the door handle. As soon as she was inside the confines of her own space, as pathetically decorated as it was, she pulled out a bottle of wine and poured a glass.

Now what the fuck was she going to do?

* * *

Landon snagged the card he'd forgotten from the top drawer of his desk and then made sure his condo was secure.

"It's really too bad about that kid," Abe said as they doubled-timed it toward the sidewalk. "But why the hell did that chick break into your place looking for answers?"

"She said something about me being in his office the last time she spoke to him."

"Have you been following the case?"

Landon shook his head. "The only thing I know is he left for work on a Friday at five. He signed out of the office and left the base, but he never made it back to his apartment, that anyone knows of, and he never showed up for work the following Monday. That was almost four weeks ago."

"Did he have any conflicts with anyone?"

A few beach stragglers raced from the ocean, laughing while they turned on the showers by the stairs and washed the sand off their feet. Landon had gone right from high school graduation to basic training where he went on a fast track to becoming a Navy SEAL. It's all he could think of since he'd turned fourteen. Abe had returned from Coronado, California, right after he'd completed his SEAL training, and Landon's mother thought it would be a good idea if she invited Abe over to talk to Landon and his friends.

That day sealed Landon's fate.

"Not that I know of," Landon said. "I really didn't know him. It's not like I was in the office all that much. Either Wyatt or Keanu always files our paperwork. The only time I go in there is when I have personal business or Wyatt makes me."

"Did you have any idea your sexy-as-fuck neighbor was his sister?"

"I'm going to tell Alabama you said that." Landon laughed.

Abe waggled his finger. "Show my wife a picture of Olympia; she'll agree with me, and you didn't answer my question."

"Not a clue. I noticed her the day she moved in and have been trying to meet her ever since. I just never expected she'd ask me for a plunger and then break into my house."

"You can't make that shit up." Abe pulled open the main door to the Sans Bar and Grill.

Landon's entire squad filled the room. Only two were married. Wyatt, his team leader, and Keanu, his task master. The rest of the crew either came solo, like Landon, or had some eye candy on their arm. This town was filled with women who wanted to say they had a SEAL for a boyfriend. Drove him crazy.

Alabama strolled across the room, leaned in, and kissed her husband. "Did you two boys have a nice little bonding excursion?"

"It was entertaining," Abe said. "I'll tell you all about it while I get myself a drink." Abe looped a protective arm around Alabama. "You want one?"

"I'll be over in a minute." Landon made his way toward the other side of the room where Wyatt leaned against the back of a stool where his pregnant wife sat. She was only about six months, but she looked like she was about to pop any day now.

Twins.

"I can't believe you two ran off and got married." He handed Wyatt the card before bending over and kissing Clover on the cheek. He'd gotten to know Clover well since he'd joined the team, and he couldn't be happier for her and Wyatt.

"If we didn't do it now, it wouldn't have been

until after these little monsters were born," Clover said, rubbing her belly. "And I didn't care about a dress or being fat or anything like that. I just wanted to make sure this one didn't get cold feet."

Wyatt held up his left hand. "I don't know if I'm going to be able to wear this on a regular basis. It's already making me nuts."

"Honey, I told you that I don't care if you never wear it." Clover slid off the chair. "I have to pee again."

Wyatt shook his head. "Every half hour, swear to God. And like five times in the middle of the night."

Landon remembered the days well; only, his late wife Linda didn't have a very good disposition about it. No. Pregnancy made her miserable. And having the baby didn't make things any better.

"Are you okay?" Wyatt asked, sipping his whiskey. "You have this perplexed look on your face."

While the only people from his team that knew about his dead wife and kid were Wyatt and Clover, Abe and his entire crew knew what had happened, but they also knew better than to bring it up. Landon almost never spoke of it. The further away he got from that horrible day, the less he blamed himself, but it still didn't change the facts.

"What can you tell me about Woodrow Anderson?" Landon asked pushing the past from his thoughts.

"The kid that manages the admin office?" Wyatt shifted his stance. "The one that went AWOL?"

"That's the one."

Wyatt shrugged. "He was transferred here maybe eight months ago. We were on a mission, but I do remember the first time we filed our after action report. I didn't have all my i's dotted or my t's crossed. He's a by-the-book lieutenant and doesn't do sarcasm well."

"There's nothing wrong with that," Landon said. "What about friends?"

"Clover and I saw him and a few of the office staff in here a couple of times." Wyatt set his glass on the counter. "What's up with the inquisition at what is basically my wedding reception and my wife's baby shower?"

Landon held up his hand. "I'm sorry. This can all wait." Out of the corner of his eye he saw his task commander, Keanu Kalen, and two of his team members, Hudson and Parker, but everyone called Parker Baby, because he was the youngest man on the squad at twenty-four.

"I hear there was some excitement at your place," Keanu said.

"Yeah, and I heard she was smoking hot," Baby said.

Wyatt gave Landon a sideways glance. "I'm lost."

"Olympia, Woodrow's brother, showed up at my place tonight looking for information about her brother. She doesn't believe he went AWOL," Landon said.

"What does she think happened?" Keanu asked.

"I didn't talk to her long enough to find out," Landon admitted. "But it's been a month, and from what I understand, Quinn hasn't a single lead, and the local police haven't done much of anything."

"If they find him, he'll be court-martialed," Wyatt said. "It's too bad; he was a nice kid. I think he was about Baby's age."

"You all do know I hate that fucking name," Baby said.

"We don't fucking care," Wyatt said with a chuckle. "You're stuck with it now."

Hudson slapped Baby's back. "At least no one will put you in a corner."

"That's such a stupid joke," Baby said behind a tight jaw. "I'm going to get a beer."

"Get me one as well, please." Landon leaned

against the railing and folded his arms. "I can't believe that nickname stuck. Now all we have to do is keep calling Lincoln 'Train' and make that stick."

"You're just lucky the nickname we tried to give you failed miserably," Wyatt said.

"That's because Rosie doesn't make any fucking sense. It's a real stretch to go from my last name Asher to 'Ring around the Rosie.'" Landon shook his head. He couldn't even remember who tried to start that one. But when this team had formed after Keanu lost his old team during a mission involving his wife that also got Clover's father killed, they all sat around after a debriefing, drinking and coming up with dumbass names.

"But Rosie matches your pretty boy face." Wyatt reached out and grabbed Landon's cheeks and shook.

Landon shoved Wyatt's hand away. "I can't wait to watch you attempt to handle two babies at once."

Wyatt puffed out his chest. "I'm going to be the baby master, you watch."

"Until they turn into toddlers," Keanu said, letting out a long breath. "Karl is approaching eighteen months, and his favorite two words are: *no dada.* He says it all day long and to everything, and he and his mother think it's cute. I can't imagine that times two."

"Isn't your wife pregnant again?" Hudson asked.

"Yeah, but by the time baby number two gets to that stage, Karl will be on to something else. Probably writing on the walls with markers." Keanu ran a hand across his face.

Baby handed Landon a beer. "I used to do that all the time," Baby said.

"Of course you did." Landon clanked his beer against Baby's. "So, where was Woodrow stationed before he came to Little Creek?"

"I don't know off the top of my head." Wyatt cocked his head. "You're not going to let this go, are you?"

"I've got a sister and two brothers. If I just up and disappeared, I hope someone would help them figure out what happened to me." Landon took a swig of his beverage and eyed the door, willing Olympia to waltz into the Sans. But he figured she probably felt humiliated, and he couldn't blame her, considering what transpired.

"Just don't piss anyone off," Keanu said.

"And let us know if we can help." Wyatt grabbed his glass from the counter. "I better go find my bride."

"I might have something for you," Baby said.

"In regard to Woodrow?"

Baby nodded. "He lived in my building. Two floors below me. We had a beer on the rooftop a couple of times. He came here from Pensacola. He's from Upstate New York, and he's not a fan of Commander Callahan."

"Seriously? Who doesn't like Callahan?" Landon and his team didn't fall under Callahan's command, but they crossed paths on more than one occasion, and he seemed like a stand-up guy. His teams respected him and had nothing but good things to say about him, so that just didn't add up.

Then again, office management had their own way of doing things, and field officers often didn't like dealing with the red tape. Keanu often complained about the redundant system, but never did so in the office. Even though he had ideas about how to make changes, it wasn't his department, and he didn't step on toes unless necessary.

"You'd be surprised," Keanu said. "He can be a real hard-ass at times."

"So can you," Hudson said. "But we still like you."

"That's what you say to my face," Keanu said with a chuckle. "What happened to the kid's apartment?"

"I honestly don't know," Baby said. "I could find out though."

"Do you mind?" Landon asked. "If it's still rented to him and not back in circulation, maybe—"

"Please tell me you don't plan on breaking into Woodrow's place?" Keanu asked.

"Nope. But I bet Olympia has access."

Keanu smacked his forehead. "I don't know what's worse. Dealing with you yahoos or dealing with a toddler who flat out enjoys defying me."

CHAPTER 2

Landon stopped at the water shower and cleaned the sand off his feet before heading across the street to his condo. Low gray clouds hugged the sky, keeping the sun from shining bright in the midmorning sky. A six-mile run on the beach was pretty good and gave him some time to clear his head. He jogged up his steps and paused, staring at his bucket with his plunger.

He scratched the back of his head and glanced toward her apartment. Was she sitting at her window watching and waiting? Well, he didn't bite, and maybe it was time they started over.

Quickly, he raced inside and shed his workout clothes, taking the fastest shower ever. He didn't bother to shave or style his extra-long flattop. He hadn't planned on doing anything today other than exercise, a little work around the condo, and then binge-watch something on the television. He might as well spend part of his day with her, helping her sort through whatever she needed to regarding her brother.

He rang her bell.

Twice.

She peeked her head out. "I returned your plunger."

"I know," he said. "Can I buy you breakfast? An early lunch? A cup of coffee? Go for a walk?"

"Why?" she asked.

"I think we got started off on the wrong foot, and I'd like to rectify that."

Pulling the door open a little wider, she stepped outside. "Considering I broke into your house, that's surprising."

"While I generally don't condone criminal activity, you had your reasons, and if it were one of my siblings, I might do the same thing." He waved his hand toward the ocean. "Why don't we go for a stroll on the beach, and I'll buy you lunch at the Sans."

"I don't know about lunch." She glanced to the sky.

"It's supposed to clear up, and I checked the

radar. There is no rain anywhere near us." He waved his hand out in front of him. "Come on. I don't bite."

"That, I don't believe." Turning, she locked her door, tugging a bungy-type bracelet with a key dangling from it up her arm. "I am sorry I broke into your house. I didn't really think that through."

"Is what you said true about the last time you talked to your brother?" He flattened his hand on the small of her back and guided her across the street. "And what exactly did he say to you?"

She had pulled her long dark hair into a braid that cascaded over her shoulder. She wore a white loose-fitting T-shirt and a pair of jean shorts that hugged her hips. She had to be close to five nine, and her legs went on forever.

"He'd called me the day before because he'd found some discrepancies in some reports for the third time by the same commander. My brother has always been a stickler for rules. Drove me nuts growing up because I wasn't a rule follower."

"How close in age are you?"

"We're twins."

"Ah. I see," he said. "But I can totally see him as a goody two-shoes."

"That he was, and I was a rebel without a cause, but he was still my best friend, and he wouldn't just take off without telling me unless something was wrong."

Or he was dead, but Landon wasn't going to voice that opinion out loud for two reasons.

First one was because the most likely cause of death would be suicide.

Second would be murder, but why? And by whom?

"Did he tell you who this commander was? Was it an actual commander, or was it a task commander or a commanding officer?"

"I don't know." She kicked off her flip-flops, holding them in her hand as she stepped onto the beach. "He never mentioned names."

Since the sun wasn't out, even though the temperature was in the eighties, not many people roamed the waterfront, which was a nice change of scenery on a Saturday. He kept the pace slow, enjoying the sand tickling his toes as the water lapped at his ankles.

He resisted the urge to take her hand. It wasn't appropriate, no matter how much he wanted to. He hadn't asked her to lunch to hit on her. His only goal was to help her figure out what happened to her twin.

"Is that because you spoke to him while he was

on base?"

"Sometimes," she said. "But even when we spoke and he was at home, he never mentioned names. He said that it would be unprofessional and against Navy policy if he were to mention names, especially when top secret missions were involved."

Landon nodded. "Your brother might have had an administrative job, but he had a high security clearance, which is why the Navy is hot to find him. He knows things that could put people like me in danger."

"Hot? It doesn't feel that way to me," she said, glaring at him. "I've spoken to that investigator you mentioned last night, and she totally blew me off."

"I'm not surprised. The Navy tends to be tight-lipped, especially during an active investigation."

"So, you believe she's searching under every rock for my brother?"

"I'm not an investigator, and I don't know how all that works, but I will go talk to her on Monday when I get to the base and see what I can find out."

"Why?" She bent over and picked up a couple of shells. "Why would you do that for me?"

"You broke into my apartment. Obviously, this is important to you, and honestly, I haven't been able to stop thinking about Woodrow since last night. I mean, it's bothered me for weeks that he just drove off the base never to be seen again. It's left a sick feeling in my gut because I don't see him as the kind of guy that would go AWOL. He loved serving his country."

"And yet, you did nothing about it."

"It wasn't my job," he said. "And it's still not. Besides, a few days after he went missing, I was sent to an undisclosed area for a mission. I was gone for ten days and only returned about the same time you moved in. But now that I'm back, I'd like to help, if I can."

The sun managed to burn through a portion of the clouds, casting a warm glow on her dark-brown hair. The breeze kicked up, brushing a few stray strands of hair across her face.

"I appreciate that." She brushed them out of the way. "I'm sorry I broke into your condo."

"Water under the bridge," he said. "What about his apartment?"

"I've already been through it, and I couldn't find anything."

"Can I ask why you didn't just stay there?"

"I thought maybe you were the high-ranking officer my brother was talking about, but I figured out pretty quickly that wasn't the case. Even so, you were the only link I had to Woodrow, so I found out where you lived and rented a place near you." There was a tremor to her voice that tugged at his heartstrings. He understood pain and loss. He knew better than most what it was like not to have real answers, or at least answers that made sense to a sane person. Regardless of the reasons for her brother's disappearance, she was hurting, and she deserved someone to really hear her and be there when nothing really added up.

Abe and Alabama had done that for him when Linda and his baby boy had died. They didn't judge Linda for what she'd done, and they didn't give him a bunch of bullshit psychobabble about what happened. No. They were just there for him and helped him through the worst time of his life.

"How the hell did you find that out?"

"The day after I found out my brother went missing, I got on a plane and came here. I went right to the Sans, and you were there. I heard someone call your name, and I followed you home. When I decided to come here, I rented the unit behind yours."

"Impressive," he said. "What's going to happen to your brother's place?"

"My parents made sure the rent and utilities

would be paid through for the next twelve months for when Woodrow came home. They are besides themselves with worry and fear, but trying to be positive, hoping that there is some logical explanation for this."

"I understand."

"How could you possibly relate to what me and my family are going through?"

He never told people about Linda or his son, Ryker. It was too painful. Even when he broached the subject with Wyatt who knew what it was like to lose a child, or Clover who was the most understanding woman in the world, it always brought Landon to his knees, making him incapable of functioning for hours.

You never got over that kind of loss.

Unless you were Wyatt and found a second chance at love.

But Wyatt's child died of cancer, and Landon's son passed under very different circumstances. Not that he was comparing pain, but the two situations did lend themselves to very different perspectives.

"I've lost people I love before."

"Who?" she asked.

"Does it matter?"

"I suppose not," she said. "But you know what

happened. Not knowing if he's dead or alive. Or if he's suffering somewhere, scared and alone. It's slowly killing my parents."

He might know how Linda and Ryker died, but he'll never understand the why, and he sure as shit wasn't going to get into it with a perfect stranger. Besides, it would only come across as if he were playing tit for tat with agony.

"You're right, I don't know what that's like. But that doesn't mean I don't have a heart," he said. "Would you be willing to take me to your brother's apartment and let me look around?"

"Why?"

"You ask that a lot." He laughed. It was actually a good single word question. If you didn't know why you were doing something, then why do it? "You're blinded by an overdose of feelings for your twin brother, which will alter your ability to see things from a clear and unbiased perspective. I don't have that kind of attachment. Plus, I know the personnel at the base; if he has anything at his place about different people, I'll know whereas you might not."

"Good point," she said. "Sure. I can take you over today or tomorrow."

"So, what is it that you do that you can rent a

relatively expensive condo and spy on me while not working?"

She laughed. It was a sweet sound that reminded him of tulips swaying in the breeze while bees buzzed about, spreading pollen from one fresh flower to the next. "That's none of your business."

"Since I've agreed to help you, I think I deserve to know if I'm dealing with a drug or arms dealer."

She jerked her head back. "Right. I work for a drug cartel in Mexico." She pursed her lips and shook her head. "I'm a freelance graphic designer so I can work from anywhere, and I'd spend my last dime to find my brother. Hell, I'd sell my body if I had to."

"Let's not go that far," he said. "I can't make any promises. I'm not a Navy cop or an investigator, and I don't know when I'll be called on a mission, but I'll do what I can to check into things."

"I will take whatever you can offer."

"And I won't even ask you for sexual favors," he said. "Now, I'm starving. Let's go get some lunch and work on a game plan."

* * *

Olympia sure as hell didn't trust Landon. He had to

have some ulterior motive for deciding to help her with tracking down what happened to her brother. Perhaps he just wanted to keep an eye on her while the Navy covered their ass.

Slipping from the driver's seat of her small SUV, she swallowed. Landon had brought his buddy Abe with him. He seemed like a nice enough fella, but kind of quiet, and he was constantly giving her the stink eye.

Honest Abe had a stick up his ass.

"How long has your brother lived here?" Abe asked.

"Almost a year. We just extended his lease for another year." She knew it sounded crazy, but without knowing, it seemed like the right thing to do. "Besides, my parents aren't ready to come down and help me go through his things. It's just too soon."

"Totally makes sense," Landon said.

She'd never had government conspiracy theory issues before, but she did now. Good men didn't just disappear without a trace. No. When that happened, it usually meant they were either dead or kidnapped and being held for some crazy reason.

Using the key fob, she entered the lobby into the tall apartment building in downtown Norfolk. Her brother had been excited when the Navy transferred him to Virginia, specifically Little Creek where he'd get to work directly with many SEAL teams, the one thing he always wanted to be, but knew he'd never make it past the training.

Her brother was mad wicked smart. Maybe too smart for his own good, but he had suffered from panic attacks when he'd been in middle school, and he also wasn't blessed with a buff body or the ability to create one. It just didn't work for him.

Of course, who was she to talk. She couldn't run to save her sorry little ass, and doing any kind of exercise class, yeah, that would be dangerous for everyone involved.

No one said a word as they rode the elevator to the sixth floor. This had been only the third time she'd been to her brother's place. The first time had been the day he moved in. The second had been a few weeks ago when she'd found out he'd gone missing. As she stood in front of his door, she took in a deep breath and let it out slowly. "I have searched his drawers, closets, desk, even looked under his mattress, so the place is a bit disheveled, and like I said, his laptop is at my condo."

"Is Baby coming down?" Abe asked.

"He said he was going to, but I think he had a chick with him when I called. He also sounded hungover as shit, and I'm pretty sure I woke him up," Landon said.

"To be young and stupid." Abe stepped into the apartment and stopped at the hallway, staring at the pictures presented on the small table. He picked up the one of Olympia and Woodrow the day Woodrow graduated from college.

"Wow," Abe said. "I didn't know he went to the Naval Academy. How hold is he?"

"Twenty-four," Olympia said.

"Baby's that age, isn't he?" Abe asked.

"Who is Baby?" Olympia asked. She really wanted to know what the hell kind of name that was, but she opted to keep that line of questions to herself.

"A member of my team who lives in this building and knows your brother." Landon made his way to the family room and started poking around.

She had to be grateful they referred to her brother in the present and not the past tense. Once people started doing that, he might as well be dead. She shivered. Deep down, she didn't want to believe that had been her brother's demise, but that was the only logical answer.

Something she had to come to terms with.

"Did your brother have a close friend in the office?" Abe asked, making his way into the kitchen which was open to the family room. "SEAL teams tend to be tighter than family, but I have no idea how the administrative staff works."

"He talked a lot about a girl by the name of Emily. He had a crush on her." She pulled down three mugs from the cabinet and made a pot of coffee. She needed to do something and since Landon had wanted to do this alone, but she wouldn't let him, she had agreed to just sit back and leave him and Abe alone.

"That would be Emily Baldwin. Sweet girl. She's basically his assistant and currently taking over his responsibilities." Landon pulled off the sofa cushions, exposing a pullout bed, something she hadn't thought of doing. "Do you know if she returned his feelings?"

"I have no idea. My brother doesn't have a lot of game when it comes to women, and without me being his wingman, he pretty much crashes and burns. However, he has no problems with girls as friends or on a professional level, so that was the plan of action, in hopes she'd make a move on him." Olympia leaned out into the hallway and watched as Abe disappeared into the bedroom. She didn't like telling Landon or his friend the details of her brother's life, but what else was she supposed to do? No one else was standing in line to help her. "I know he occasionally met her out for breakfast before heading into work. I think she might have lived around here. He also talked about a Greg Brody and a Finn Walker."

"I know Finn," a new male voice said.

Olympia jumped, sloshing coffee down the front of her shirt. "Shit," she mumbled.

"Sorry," the young man with a ridiculous baby-face said. "I'm Parker—"

"His name is Baby." Landon smacked him on the back.

"And you're an asshole," Baby said as he took one of the mugs of coffee. "Sorry about that." He pointed to her shirt." But thanks for this."

"You're welcome," she said, wiping down the coffee mess.

"You must be Olympia. Your brother speaks very highly of you." Baby leaned against the counter while Landon joined Abe in her brother's room. She probably should be back there with them, but she'd promised Landon she'd stay out of his way unless asked.

"I'm sorry, I don't think my brother ever mentioned you."

"Well, I only had a couple of beers with him. We

didn't socialize in the same circles." Baby opened up a couple of cabinets, examining the plates and glasses, pushing them aside.

She had no idea what any of them were looking for, but they certainly covered places she hadn't thought of. "When did you hang out with him last?"

"Maybe four months ago? We were sitting on the rooftop blowing off steam and having a few drinks."

Landon reappeared in the kitchen. "Anyone else there?"

"Yeah, Finn," Baby said. "He used to live in this building too, but he moved two months ago."

"Where'd he move to?" Landon asked.

"In with his girlfriend across town," Baby said.

"Found something." Abe strolled into the tiny kitchen holding a key chain with one key dangling from it. "It was tucked behind the toilet."

"I would never think to look there," Olympia admitted, holding her hand out.

Abe placed the key in her hand. "It looks like a key to a safety deposit box. Do you know where he does his banking?"

"All that information is in his bedroom in the filing cabinet next to his desk," she said.

Abe shook his head. "After I found the key, I went looking in those drawers, and they are empty."

"That's impossible." Olympia slammed her mug on the counter and shoved Landon aside as she raced toward her brother's bedroom. "I was just here a couple of weeks ago, and I went through all his stuff. The only thing I took with me was his computer." Her heart beat so fast she thought it might pound right out of her chest. She reached for the drawer, pulling it open slowly, and gasped. She thumbed through what files were left, which were his renters' insurance, car insurance, and his medical information, but all his bank records were gone. "That's weird. They were here. I know they were because I checked his last statement."

"Was there anything weird in the bank accounts?" Lincoln asked.

"No. I mean, he has more money than I thought he would, but he was always good at saving."

"How much more?" Abe asked. "An unusual amount? Was there a large deposit or something?"

"No." She shook her head giving Abe a nasty glare. "I was surprised he hadn't moved what he had in his checking to either a savings or an investment account. He was always on me about investing and having my money work for me, but I tend to spend whatever I bring in." She went through the bottom drawer as well as all the drawers in his desk. "What if other things are missing? I mean he was a huge reader, and I don't see a book on his nightstand. He read every night before he went to sleep."

"Okay, but what would someone want with bank accounts and books?" Baby asked, sitting on the edge of the bed.

"If, and this is just for argument's sake, Woodrow was taking bribes or selling top secret information, that might show up in his bank accounts." Landon had the nerve to rest his hands on her shoulders as if he cared or for support or something to make up for his ugly accusation.

"If that were the case, why would someone steal them?" She shrugged his hands off her body. "Wouldn't they want to call attention to something like that? Show that my brother was a traitor?"

"Not if it linked it back to whoever took them," Abe said. "But I've met your brother, and while I've seen a lot of shit in my day, and even good people have a trigger that will send them down a path no would could see coming, your brother wouldn't be involved in anything illegal. Not by choice."

"Wait a minute." She brushed her wild hair from her face. "You're not stationed here, so how do you know my brother?"

"My team has done some special ops with

Landon's squad, which has brought me to the base," Abe said. He had this calmness about him that probably made most people feel safe. It just drove Olympia crazy. "Your brother is a stickler for detail, something I admire in a man."

"Come on, Abe." Landon leaned against the doorjamb. "We both know that good people do bad things. We've both seen people we thought were one of the good guys turn over a bad leaf."

"Woodrow would never." She poked Landon in the forearm. "Some commander was giving him a hard time about something. It was so bad that he couldn't talk about the specifics, but he was scared, and he told me so."

"Scared how?" Baby asked. "Because even though Woodrow often seemed like a pushover, no one took advantage of him. He might have been a nerd, so to speak, but he was still a badass. That's what Wyatt would say."

"I would agree with that statement," Abe said. "But you know your brother better than we do. What are your thoughts?"

She tossed her hands wide. "The only thing I know is that my brother was upset over some commander, and he couldn't talk about it. He seemed a little off the last few times I spoke to him, and my parents said he wasn't as quick to return calls and texts. He seemed preoccupied the last few weeks before his disappearance."

"You mentioned you had his computer?" Landon asked.

She nodded. "But none of his obvious passwords are working, so I haven't been able to get into it."

"Moon should be able to crack it," Baby said.

"Who is Moon?" Olympia asked.

"Another buddy of ours," Landon said. "He's a bit of a computer genius. If you don't mind, I can see if he can come over tomorrow and check it out."

"Okay." When Olympia had packed up what few things she owned, and moved out of her furnished apartment, she hadn't really formulated a game plan to figure out what happened to Woodrow. Her brother used to lecture her on her inability to organize, much less formulate any goals and execute them. He always told her that flying by the seat of her pants was fine when she'd been in high school, and maybe in the first year or two of college, but after that, it wasn't going to help her be successful in any career or relationship.

But she hadn't taken that path and Woodrow hadn't a clue what she had to do in order to survive until it was almost too late.

"Alabama and I are only here until tomorrow afternoon, but Cookie, Benny, and I are coming back next week for a couple of days, so I can continue to do some digging. We'll also get Tex in on this."

"Thanks. I appreciate that," Landon said. "I'd like to set up some kind of video motion sensor inside this apartment. If someone broke in, they might come back, especially if they were looking for that key."

"I can take care of that today," Baby said.

"All right then," Landon said. "We've got our work cut out for us."

Woodrow had always told Olympia that sailors weren't like every day normal people. That his brothers-and sisters-in-arms were loyal to the bone. And maybe these men were, but she couldn't shake the idea that someone on that base hurt her brother.

CHAPTER 3

Olympia stood on her front patio and soaked in the warm morning sun as she sipped her hot tea. She'd gotten maybe three hours of sleep between trying to keep up with her workload so she didn't lose her current client base and worrying about her brother and the fact that he was most likely dead.

It wasn't some weird twin connection that made her believe the worst. She hadn't had some cosmic connection with Woodrow, though they did have an uncanny ability to read each other's mind. Not literally, but they were in tune with each other and understood each other in ways no one else ever could, even their parents. But it wasn't like she felt her brother's pain or sensed when he was in trouble.

Unless she heard it in his voice, and that last time she'd spoken to him, he'd been spooked.

Landon stepped from his apartment wearing only his jeans, which weren't buttoned at the top. He held a travel mug in one hand and what looked like a plate of pastries. His sexy bare feet carried him across the wood planks. "Good morning," he said, holding out the tray of two muffins. "Both blueberry, both homemade, both loaded with calories."

She laughed. Setting her mug on the railing, she took a tasty treat. She picked at it with her fingers and plopped a chunk into her mouth, pleasantly surprised by the bursting rich flavor of berries and sugar with a hint of what she thought might be cream cheese filling her taste buds. "These are really good."

"And really bad for you, but it's my weekend ritual."

"Are all sailors superstitious?" She adjusted her five-dollar folding beach chairs she'd picked up at the local grocery store and offered him a seat. She wished she had contacts or at least knew someone like a private investigator that she could ask to look into Landon's background. She'd learned a long time ago that people who were too good to be true, were exactly that. Landon came on a little too strong in his willingness to help, as did the rest of his buddies.

Her brother's voice tickled the back of her mind. From the moment he stepped foot on the Naval Academy campus, he knew he'd found his home. His eyes would light up like Christmas trees when he spoke about his brothers-in-arms. As his twin, she understood the unique bond, but it was difficult to comprehend the blind trust these men and women had for each other, especially when she knew one of them was responsible for her brother's disappearance.

"Many are, but my little muffin routine isn't being superstitious. It's just something I've been doing for a long time. It's a habit, and I'm not going to go into shock if I don't do it." His terse tone seemed a little over the top for the conversation, but she wasn't about to start a hot discussion over that. "Was your brother superstitious? Or have any rituals or odd habits?"

Well, she set herself up for that line of questioning. "He liked to make pulled pork on Sunday during football season, and whenever he watched the Sabres play hockey, he had to have his stupid knee hockey stick in his hand. But nothing that was so outrageous that he'd freak out if it didn't happen."

"But he was rigid when it came to rules." Landon took a long sip from his mug. Either he had a perpetual five o'clock shadow, or he hadn't shaved that morning. He hadn't a single hair on his chest, and his stomach muscles were well defined, but he wasn't overtly muscular. Tall, long, and lean.

"You say that like you know it as a well-documented fact."

"My buddy Abe, one of his old members is a master at finding out things as well as finding people. We gave him your brother's name, and he started working his magic."

She narrowed her eyes. Heat prickled her skin like a porcupine. "My brother didn't do anything wrong. He's the one who is missing."

Landon held up his hands as if someone were holding a gun to his head. "I'm well aware of that fact. However, we have nothing to go on, so looking into your brother, his past inside the Navy, and out, might give us a better perspective on why he might disappear. I'm on your side, or why would I even bother?"

"To cover up your crime."

He curled his fingers around his metal beverage container and stood. "I understand you're upset and scared, and all you want to do is find Woodrow. I get it. I really do. I'm giving up my free time to help, and I don't have to do that. I don't know you, and I barely knew your brother. If, or when, you want to have a constructive conversation, come knock on my door."

"Wait," she said, letting out a long breath. "I'm sorry. While I didn't really mean it, I can't help but think about the last time I spoke to Woodrow. He was spooked, and you came into the office, and he had to go. He promised he called me later, and he never did."

Landon leaned against the side of the building. "And did you try to call him? Because it was a few days after that before he disappeared."

"I called and left him a message, and he texted me back saying he was really busy and he'd call me when things calmed down. Any idea what he was busy with?"

Landon shook his head. "I've never met anyone who's never received a single demerit in a military school."

"Did you go to the Naval Academy?"

He nodded. "But I'm about six years older than you and Woodrow. So, I didn't know him there, and yes, I managed a few demerits." He laughed. "More than a few. But Tex said Woodrow's school record was impeccable. The cleanest boy-next-door nerd."

"That's the best description of Woodrow that I've ever heard, and its one of the reasons he wanted to join the military. He likes structure."

"And what about you?"

"Fuck no," she said, dunking her muffin into her coffee and tossing the moist cake like a treat into her mouth. It really was the best muffin she'd ever had. "I really hate routine. It's why I lasted less than five minutes working for someone else and I ended up going solo. I can work at three in the morning if I want to, as long as I get the work done."

"What is it you do again?"

"I'm a graphic artist and photographer. I do a lot of book covers, album covers, creative advertising for social media, shit like that."

"Is there good money in that?" he asked. His blue eyes caught the sunrays, brightening the color to match the sea, but there was an intenseness to them that intimidated her, making her wonder if she'd picked the right man. During the few weeks she had been watching him, she noted his serious nature, but it wasn't anything like Woodrow, who just liked things to be nice and neat. Woodrow believed everything had a place, and he enjoyed writing policy and procedural manuals for even the simplest of tasks.

Woodrow was a geek in the truest sense of the word, but he wasn't a loner.

Landon might be part of one of the tightest teams in the Navy, but if there was ever a poster child for a lone wolf, it would be Landon.

"I probably would do better if I had stayed longer at a big company, but now that I have a steady flow of clients, I'm doing well enough." She waggled her finger. "That's one of the few areas my brother and I saw eye to eye on."

"What's that?"

"I'm not cut out to take orders from anyone."

"Good to know," he said, running his hand over the side of his head. "Did you know your brother failed both the physical and the psychological test for SEAL training?"

"I did." She turned her gaze toward the ocean. She'd begged her brother not to go down that slippery slope. A lot of his little OCD quirks accelerated when he went to college. He'd learned to manage them, and most people wouldn't notice his tapping in sets of threes, but in his stress situations, it became noticeable to the world around him, and sometimes, it could overwhelm him.

"How did he feel about that?"

"He knew he'd fail. But he thought it was the best way to get close to the elite group of sailors and find a way to work with them," she said behind a tight jaw. Woodrow had planned out his entire life, and he'd made it happen. He always managed to overcome his character flaws. Hell, even though he had absolutely no game when it came to women, his plan had him married with kids by the time he was thirty, and she figured he would make that happen one way or the other.

That was just Woodrow's way.

"He could have just talked to his CO. He's more than qualified for his post."

"But Woodrow wanted to at least have a taste of SEAL life. He thought that would make the files he dealt with real people, not ink on paper, especially when he's often redacting information when outsiders demand information. He kind of got off on doing that." She rubbed her temple. She would never understand why he enjoyed that so much. The military was filled with secrets and lies.

"When he did that, he protected people like me. There are things we do that just don't need to be in the public eye."

"But my brother's disappearance does, and the

Navy isn't talking. I've taken it to reporters; I've posted on social media, but I get no response from the Navy other than standard bullshit and a request to stop talking about it publicly. I'm sure you can see how that might make me think the Navy is covering something up."

"I can," Landon said. "But the military is constantly dealing with top secret missions that if the media were to report on them, it could put many lives in danger. That said, I put a call into Quinn. I'm hoping she calls me back today. If not, I'll see her on base tomorrow."

"What makes you think she'll tell you any more than she's told me?"

"She probably won't, but I'll be able to read between the lines. She'll also be advised that me and my team are looking into it, and that might make her change the way she's doing things. She might use us, and that can only help you find out what happened."

A man driving a convertible Volkswagen Beetle parked in the space next to Landon's Harley. He smiled, showing off a set of pearly white teeth. He wore bright-pink Bermuda shorts and a white-and-pink long-sleeved sun shirt. Bending over, the man snagged a bag from the back seat of the car.

"Hey, Moon." Landon pushed from the side of the condo. "Thanks for coming over."

"Only plans I had today were with my sofa and Netflix." Moon looked like he should be spending his weekends at a posh country club with some chick by the name of Buffy hanging on his arm like she'd just won the catch of the county.

"Moon, this is Olympia."

Olympia stretched out her hand. "I appreciate your help."

"My pleasure,' Moon said. "If you don't mind, I'd like to set up in Landon's place."

"No problem. I'll go get my brother's computer, but I'm not letting you take it, so I'm coming with you. And staying."

"Didn't expect anything less," Landon said. "My door will be unlocked; no need to climb through a window."

"For the record, I also unlocked the sliders, and that's how I got in."

Landon shook his head. "Use the front door, please."

* * *

"That's an angry woman."

Landon glared at Moon. "She's just upset because her twin brother is missing. How do you think you'd behave if it were Ria that had gone AWOL?"

"That might put me in a bad mood." Moon set up some equipment on the kitchen table. "Once I'm in, Baby's going to patch in remotely, and we're going to internally flag what we can so if anyone does anything to Woodrow's laptop, even if from a distance, we'll know about it."

"I feel like a shit for not trusting her, but something tells me she's not being totally up front with me."

"You're not being honest with her, and Abe's having a field day with that one." Moon laughed.

"Hey, I didn't know about where the investigation was going until late last night." Landon hated feeding her half-truths and in some cases down and outright lies. But until they knew more about Woodrow, and his twin, that's how it was going to have to be.

"But you've asked all of us to act as if we haven't heard the worst." Moon glanced over one of his gadgets. "Honest Abe crinkled and snubbed his nose to that one."

Landon chuckled. "He did not."

"I haven't met all of Wyatt and Keanu's old

buddies, but they are quite the crew, and Abe is quirkier than Lincoln and Bryce with their obsession with all things Marvel."

"You know I grew up down the street from Abe. I've known him since I was like eight."

"I didn't know that," Moon said. "But it makes sense. You've got about the best resting bitch face as anyone I've ever met. Must have been in the water you and he were drinking."

Landon had heard it all before, but the worst of it came from his family, especially his sister Grace. Ever since Linda and Ryker died, Grace had told him he'd lost his smile as well as the sparkle that beamed from his eyes like a headlight cutting through the fog. She was constantly trying to shove pictures in his face, comparing him when Linda was alive to the last few years.

Problem with doing that was he could see the light in his life fade long before Linda had taken her own. He just hid it better back then.

"Not everyone wears their emotions on their sleeve." Landon kept his focus on the front door, which he'd left wide open, letting the warm ocean breeze filter through the screen, allowing him to hear her footsteps on the wood patio as she made it from her place to his. "Be honest with me; do you think I should tell her any part of what we've found?"

"Everyone liked her brother. But if what Tex dug up and what Callahan is confirming, she's in for a rude awakening."

"That doesn't answer my question."

Moon leaned over and plugged something into the wall. "It wouldn't be a good idea. Not yet anyway."

"I'm just really struggling to believe Tex's theory."

"Well, if his bank accounts are drained, you can bet your bottom dollar that where Quinn is taking the investigation is probably right on the money."

"I wish she would hurry up and call me back. We don't have confirmation that she's actually going in that direction," Landon said.

"I've only met this Tex dude once, but are you really questioning his intel?" Moon had a point. Tex would have stated he was making an educated guess about the investigation, but no, Tex had made it quite clear that they absolutely believed Woodrow was alive and well and responsible for the sale of highly classified mission briefs."

The sound of a spring-loaded door slamming into a wood frame echoed in the morning air.

Olympia scurried across the front patio carrying

a laptop along with a notebook and a pair of black framed glasses pushed on top of her head.

Moon and Baby were whiz kids when it came to electronics, and Landon had complete faith that Moon would not only be able to crack the password, but once he got inside, Moon would find his way through a back end opening. Whether they found anything or not, they would have eyes on and in the machine.

"Here you go." Olympia handed Landon the computer. "And here is a list of passwords I've already tried and some word and word combinations that are meaningful to Woodrow."

"Thanks." Moon took both the list and the computer. "That might help me set some parameters on my password cracking program." He settled at the kitchen table and went about his work.

Landon knew better than to bother him, but Olympia stood just a few feet behind him, gnawing on her thumbnail. "Do you want more coffee? Tea? Water? Another muffin?"

She shook her head and didn't budge.

Moon glanced over his shoulder and then quickly at Landon before flipping open the computer and hitting the power button.

"Why don't we give Moon some room to work."

Olympia took one tiny step back.

Not exactly what he had in mind.

Moon let out a puff of air as he inserted a flash drive in the USB port and tapped a few keystrokes on the keyboard.

Olympia inched closer, blinking as the computer screen lit up. "You're in?"

"Not yet. I'm just setting up the parameters to run my program. It could take anywhere from five minutes to a couple of hours." Moon leaned back and folded his arms over his chest.

"That's it. That's all you're going to do?" Olympia asked.

"Is she always this pessimistic?" Moon asked.

"I wouldn't know. I just met her a couple of days ago." Landon reached out and squeezed her shoulder, all of a sudden painfully aware all he had on was his jeans.

And he'd forgotten to button them.

"I'm not totally clueless to technology. I took a fair amount of programing classes in college. I would think you need write all sorts of code and—"

"I did all that before I came over here," Moon said. "And I wrote this program with one of the best ethical hackers in the world. Even the CIA and the FBI hires out my friend. So—fuck," Moon said, yanking out the tiny external drive. He pressed his finger on the power button until the computer shut down, and then he yanked the main cord from the socket. "That's not good."

"What the hell is wrong?" Landon asked.

"Someone put a tracer on the computer, and the moment it connects to Wi-Fi, like it did when my program found the password, it alerts whoever set it up in the first place." Moon tapped his fingers on the screen of his tablet. "Does your brother possess exceptional computer skills?"

"He knows his way around writing a good macro in a spreadsheet," she said. "But I'm not really following what you're talking about, so I doubt my brother could do it. Then again, I'm not exactly sure I understand what his job is with the Navy."

"I'm sure Landon can explain that to you." Moon packed up his belongings. "We weren't on long enough for whoever bugged that thing to get an exact location, but they will be able to see that the computer was activated within about a thirty-mile radius." He held up the laptop. "You're going to have to trust us and let me take this. We can't lead whoever is tracking it to yours and Landon's front door."

"But what if it's my brother?" she asked.

"That's a valid question." Landon quickly made sure his pants were buttoned while he found his shirt and pulled it over his head before looping his arm around Olympia. For as much as he questioned her honesty, he felt a draw toward her that he couldn't resist. He believed to his core that whatever she kept from him wasn't a horrible secret that would end up proving her or her brother to be traitors, but simply something she wasn't ready to share yet.

That was something he could understand.

Every girl he dated ended up dumping him after a month or so and not because of his deployments, but because he didn't share his deep and darkest secrets.

Well, it wasn't a secret, but it wasn't something he could discuss with a woman while cuddling after sex. Hell, it wasn't a conversation he could have with anyone at any given time. It just never seemed appropriate.

And it always shocked people into speechlessness or pity.

He hated both.

"I don't know under what circumstance he'd do that," Moon said. "But I'm thinking we get this piece of equipment to Tex ASAP."

Olympia shook her head wildly. "No. I don't want to part with it."

"It's the only way we're going to not only be able to gain access to your brother's computer, but find exactly who installed the tracker. We're not the enemy," Moon said.

"I don't know that."

"Just take it," Landon said. He was done playing Mr. Sympathetic. "Let's go outside while Moon packs up." He curled his fingers around her firm forearm.

"Let go of me." She jerked free. "Who the fuck do you think you are?"

"The man you came to for help, that's who." He flattened his hand on the small of her back and gave her a little shove. "Now, don't make me ask you twice to go outside."

"You're an asshole," she mumbled.

"No. I'm not. I'm just acting like one because you bring it out in me," he said behind a clenched jaw. It was rare that he ever lost his patience with a lady, but Olympia had done nothing but act like a brat since the moment she broke into his apartment, and it was time to set the record straight. He took her by the hand and practically dragged her out of his apartment. He double-timed it to her condo and pushed open the door.

The tenants that rented before her had been a young professional couple, about the same age as Landon. The owners kept the place scarcely decorated, but tasteful and in keeping with the beach feel.

"Stop manhandling me."

"I will when you stop acting like a child."

She stomped into the kitchen and pulled out a bottle of champagne and cranberry juice. "It's five o'clock somewhere and mimosas are a breakfast beverage. Want one?"

"Don't mind if I do." He didn't generally drink during the day, but he could use one right about now.

"I'm sorry, but I'm struggling to trust you because I don't believe what you're telling me. I think you're either lying to me or keeping something from me."

"And why do you say that?" Landon asked as he made himself comfortable on the barstool in front of the galley kitchen. "I've done nothing but help you since you showed up."

"Because I got this text this morning." She set her cell on the counter in front of him. "I don't recognize the number."

He lifted her phone and stared at the screen.

757-703-2321: You went to the wrong man for help. He's part of the problem, and he will lead you away from your brother, not toward him.

At least she didn't respond, but this text added a whole new dimension to the situation. He shot Tex a message and copied Abe, Wyatt, and Keanu with the text and the number. Tex should be able to find out who that number belonged to, though Landon suspected if the person who sent it had half a brain, the number belonged to a burner phone.

"So, we're being watched." He stood, making his way to the picture window that overlooked Beach Road and the ocean. "And whoever is responsible for your brother's disappearance, or knows what happened, doesn't want me helping." He glanced over his shoulder. "There are some things I haven't told you, but you haven't leveled with me either. So, as soon as my buddy leaves, why don't we both lay all our cards on the table." He turned, holding up his finger. "However, I have to be careful with top secret information."

"I think I can live with that," she said.

"And we need to let Moon look at your phone."

The sound of knuckles tapping at the screen door caught Landon's attention. Moon stood in the doorway.

Landon waved him in, holding out her cell.

"Why am I looking at her phone?" Moon asked.

"She got a bizarre text," Landon said, holding up the cell.

Moon took it, taking a screenshot. "I'm going to text this to myself. Mind if I poke around in your phone for a few minutes?"

"Actually, I do. I have private things on it." She mixed the mimosas and poured two glasses, holding one out to Moon, who shook his head.

Landon gladly took the beverage and downed half of it in one gulp. Everything about this situation gave him heartburn.

"I'm going to head over the hotel where Abe, Cookie, Benny, and Mozart are staying. I know they are all leaving today, so I want to discuss all this with them before they go since they all plan on helping." Moon set the phone on the counter.

"Thanks. I appreciate it," Landon said, holding the door open for his buddy. "I'll talk to you soon." He closed the door and turned to face Olympia. "You talk first."

CHAPTER 4

Olympia poured a second mimosa before sitting on the blue-and-white striped sofa and kicking up her feet, resting them on the matching ottoman in front of the fireplace. There had been five apartments available for rent in this building, and this one had been by far the nicest and the most expensive. All that was required was for her to sign a minimum of a six-month lease, and since she didn't own much to begin with, she opted to put what worldly possessions she did have in a small storage facility until her brother was found and she figured out what the fuck was next.

She dropped her head back and closed her eyes. The cushion next to her sank. Warmth transferred from Landon's body to hers.

Why did he have to sit so close?

The only reason she ended up being such a bitch to him half the time was because every time she looked at him, all she wanted to do was curl up in a ball, snuggle up next to him, and let it all out. He made her feel safe when her mind was scattered and she couldn't make sense of anything. He had a cool, easy demeanor, and while his friend might be called *Honest Abe,* Landon should have the nickname of *Pa* or *Charles Ingles* because he just had that kindness that the character portrayed on the television show.

"I'm waiting," Landon said.

She inhaled sharply, letting it out with a harsh blow. "Five days before my brother disappeared, he randomly transferred fifty thousand dollars into an offshore account in my married name," she said.

"Married? You're married?"

"I'm a widow, but that's not important," she said, wondering why he got hung up on that concept. The issue at hand was her brother, not her late husband. "Woodrow told me it was blood money and that if he disappeared, I should just take the money and use it to pay off debt or help Mom and Dad or buy a damn boat if I wanted. He said it was untraceable and that if he was gone, it wouldn't matter."

"Wait a second." Landon tapped her shoulder.

She blinked open her eyes.

"What did he say about the money if he didn't disappear?"

"He said it would be proof of what the high-ranking officer was doing. Something about making this man feel like Woodrow was finally caving to his demands. He said he had a plan and that he had help." She turned, tucking her foot under her butt. "But I honestly don't know who might be helping him. I thought maybe you could have gone either way."

"I wasn't helping him, but maybe the chick from the office was. I'll go talk to her on Monday."

Olympia knew she was pushing her luck, but she was desperate. "Any chance you could bring me on base as a guest? Let me walk around, talk to people?"

"I'll bring you to the base, but not to poke around," he said. "You'll have to trust me and play things my way, okay?"

"That's not going to be an easy task for me," she said. "I don't follow directions well, and I certainly don't take orders from anyone."

He chuckled. "That's good to know." He tossed his arm over the back of the sofa and sipped his drink, staring out at the ocean. "So, let me get this straight. He gave you money in an offshore account that you were to hold for him until he could use it to prove this Navy officer was doing something bad, but if he didn't come back, the money was yours to do what you wanted."

"That's basically it."

"I find that hard to be believe," Landon said.

"Why?" She glared out him.

"Because Woodrow is a rule follower. If he was trying to take someone down, but had to do it through back channels, that's already out of his comfort zone. I would guess if he's willing to break his own code, wouldn't he want, and expect, you to finish what he started?"

"That depends on what it was and if he thought I had a fighting chance on completing it successfully," she admitted. "I don't know jack shit about the Navy, and when I offered to come for a visit right before he went AWOL, he was adamant I stay out of it. He used the word dangerous at least half a dozen times." She let out a long breath. "I told you what I was holding back. Now it's your turn."

"My buddy Tex has uncovered some damaging information that points to your brother selling top secret intel on missions overseas."

She opened her mouth to protest, but he shushed her by pressing his index finger firmly over her lips.

"I don't know if Quinn, the investigator, has uncovered this as well, but if she hasn't, she will soon. Mostly likely Monday morning at the latest. What that potentially means is that your brother is alive, but a traitor."

"He's not a traitor," she said behind gritted teeth as she curled her fingers around Landon's wrists. "He used the words high-ranking officer and commander when it came to the person giving him a hard time. What does that mean?"

"Well, I'm a lieutenant. I'm a ranking officer, but I'm not that high up. The next rank is a lieutenant commander and then a commander. But there are other titles that have commander attached to it, like task commander. That's my team leader. His name is Keanu. He heads up two eight-person squads. His rank doesn't coincide with his title, so it gets confusing. And when I move up in the ranks, it might only have more to do with pay, than my job because I doubt I'll leave being the maritime person on a SEAL squad. I don't see the point."

"I think I follow all that."

"I want you to take some time and think through all the conversations you've had with your brother, maybe even write down the terms he used, and then I'll go over them, looking for clues."

"I can do that," she said. "But it wasn't until the last few weeks before he disappeared that he started to tell me anything."

"How long had you been worried about him?"

"Maybe two months before that. He seemed distant, and he didn't always respond to my texts as fast as he normally did. At first, I was hoping it was because he was making nicey-nice with Emily, but then he started telling me how scared he was."

"And he never once gave you a name."

"Just yours."

Landon rubbed his temples. "That's a little different from what you told me before."

"I know. I'm sorry," she said. "This is all new territory for me."

"Did you go to the police?"

Boy, had that been a nightmare. "I did. But they won't do anything."

"It's Navy business, and I'm sure Quinn has made that clear."

"I can't say that made me feel like the military was doing everything they could." She sipped her drink. Unfortunately, the alcohol had gone right to her head and she'd caught a nice little buzz, but it made the room sway back and forth as if she were floating out at sea. "It felt more like a cover-up."

"No. But I will give you secretive, and there are reasons for that. Whether you agree with them or not, they save the lives of the men and women risking theirs every day for you."

"You sound like my brother," she mumbled, pulling up her cell. "Here's my last few text messages with him. To paraphrase, he told me that the less I knew, the safer it was for me and that I should delete the texts and any communication I had with him that mentioned he had any concerns."

"And did you?"

She shook her head. "Like I said, I don't follow direction well."

Landon jumped to his feet. "I'm going to need to see everything. And I mean everything. And I want it right now."

She rubbed her forehead. Her brother had thrived on schedules and rituals, and her parents weren't any different. It created an environment that almost enabled her brother's OCD and yet at the same time hid it from the world. But for Olympia, all the rules and regulations drove her right into the arms of Mr. Wrong.

"I need you to do me a favor. It's going to sound potentially stupid to you, but it's important to me," she said.

"All right." Landon stood over her with his hands on his hips.

"Please don't bark orders at me or make demands. I will dig my heels into the sand and do the exact opposite, as childish as that sounds. It's my defense mechanism when I feel backed into a corner or get scared."

"I will work on my delivery in instances like this," he said. "But if we find ourselves in a situation where bullets are flying, then I will be making demands, and I will expect you to follow them."

"Fair enough." She took the hand he offered. "You have the texts on my phone, and if you go to my email, just search Woodrow and all of his will pop up. Just please don't look at anything else. It's not your business."

"Now you make me wonder if there is something you're hiding on your phone."

"I am." She patted his chest and felt a moan bounce off the back of her throat as his tight muscles flexed under her touch. "There are naked selfies on that cell."

"Jesus, you shouldn't have said that," he mumbled. "I should tell you that I was never a Boy Scout."

"If you go through my pictures, you might end up a Girl Scout." Her brother had told her when Conrad died and she'd been cleared of all suspicion that she should delete the evidence of what that monster had done to her, but she preferred to keep it as a constant reminder that being defiant nearly got her killed.

* * *

Sunday had been long and hard, which was a far cry from a day of rest.

Landon tapped his cell and pulled up a text from Tex.

Tex: I found some information on Olympia and her late husband you should know.

Landon: Related to her missing brother?

Tex: Doesn't appear to be, but it might give you some insight into what you're dealing with. That chick has been through some shit.

Landon: What kind of shit?

Tex: The kind of bad stuff that changes a person's soul.

There were a lot of things that turned a person upside down, giving them a new perspective. However, there were a few life-changing events that would forever stain a person's heart. Landon knew all too well what that could do to a person's psyche.

He had to constantly keep his in check because straddling the past with the present was a tough place to live.

But it was his only reality and the only thing keeping him sane.

Landon: Any other intel about Woodrow?

Tex: Waiting for the computer to come to me. I'll have it tomorrow, and I'll know more then too.

Landon: Thanks for the help.

Tex: Anytime. Check your email. If you have questions, I might have answers. I'm still doing a deep dive.

Tapping on the icon, Landon found the message from Tex and clicked on the first attachment. He swallowed as he stared at an image of Olympia battered and beaten. The headline read: *Woman kills Marine after living a two-year nightmare.*

He reached out and traced her bruised face. Both her eyes were nearly swollen shut. From the image, he couldn't even tell what color they were.

He scrolled down to the rest of the article.

Thirty-two-year-old Marine Conrad Keto died last month in what was originally thought to be a murder at the hands of his wife, twenty-year-old Olympia Anderson. However, after a thorough investigation, it has been ruled that Ms. Anderson acted in self-defense after her husband beat her. There were two eyewitnesses that can corrobo-

rate her story. Ms. Anderson further alleges that for two years, her husband repeatedly abused her and kept her hostage, but that hasn't been proven.

"Jesus," Landon whispered. He rubbed his aching temples. It amazed Landon, and frankly terrified him, what Tex could find out about a person with what little information he'd been given.

The article about her late husband had been disturbing, but the image of her battered body had been worse. Landon glanced over his shoulder. Olympia lay on the sofa, on her side with her knees slightly bent and her hand tucked under her cheek. The sound of some reality television show filled the room with white noise.

She was only twenty-five years old, and to think at twenty she had to literally claw her way out of an abusive marriage, and to a man who had been much older. He scanned the article again. She'd only been eighteen when she'd gotten married, which meant her husband had been thirty. That bordered on child abuse.

He picked up his cell.

Landon: What else do you know?

Tex: His family managed a gag order. That's the most comprehensive news report we have.

Landon: That's pathetic.

Tex: I know. I'm pulling some strings to see if I can't get copies of the police reports.

"How late are you going to stay here?" Olympia sat up and stretched her arms up over head. "It's getting late, and don't you have to go to work in the morning?"

"I do, but either I'm sleeping here, or you're sleeping at my place."

She narrowed her stare. "That's not going to happen because bullets aren't flying."

"I can ask you nicely, if you want, but it's not going to change that you shouldn't be alone. You can even kick me out, but then I'll just pull out my cot and catch a few z's on your front patio."

"You wouldn't dare."

"Try me." He leaned back and folded his arms across his chest.

"And what are you going to do when you're at work? Who's going to be my babysitter then?"

"A security camera, find my iPhone, and a few friends."

"I don't think so." She made her way to the front door and pulled it open. "I'm a grown woman who can protect herself."

"I read that about you." Motherfucker. Why the

hell would he go and say something as stupid as that. He stood.

"Excuse me?" She slammed the door closed so hard it rattled the wall, knocking over a seashell picture. "You read what about me?"

"Nothing."

"Oh no, you don't." She closed the gap in four quick steps and poked him dead center in the chest.

He rubbed his skin and stared up at her dark eyes glowing a fiery red.

"You and your friends obviously dug up my sordid past, so bring on the judgments. Condemn me to being a horrible person who upset her husband, pushing him over the edge, and then used that as an excuse to murder a decorated Marine."

"What?" He blinked. "That is so not where I was going with that."

"Really? Because all you military guys stick together. Did you know, even at first, Woodrow questioned what happened? My own brother didn't believe me."

"Okay. Let's calm down and take a deep breath."

"You want me to calm down? Do you have any idea what it's like to be called a murderer when all you did was fight to stay alive?" she pleaded with him with tears trickling down her cheeks. "And then be told you're not allowed to talk about it? I would go out in public and reporters would shove their damn microphones in my face, and I couldn't say one damn fucking word to defend my actions or tell everyone what a monster Conrad was. I'm still not allowed to."

"I have no idea what that would be like," he admitted. "But if it's any consolation, based on the information that was presented to me, I believe you did what you had to." He reached across the counter and pulled up the tablet. "I only read this article." He handed it to her. "But the photograph says it all."

She held the electronic device in her trembling hands. She shoved it at his chest. "You have no idea."

"Why don't you enlighten me?"

"Because it has nothing to do with my brother going missing."

"But it has everything to do with the way you handle situations."

"Oh, what? Are you afraid I'm going to kill you now too?" she asked with venom dripping off every word. She scuffed off to the kitchen and uncorked a bottle of red wine, pouring two small glasses.

That was nice of her, and he gladly took it.

He realized he was really going to have to choose his words carefully around her, but he also needed to know the full extent of what happened. He needed to know her triggers, because she clearly hadn't dealt with everything that had transpired.

And he understood that.

He had to learn to hide his triggers because his job demanded it. No one needed a Navy SEAL who loses his shit when he was supposed to be calm, cool, and collected. But he had years of training and he hadn't been abused.

By the anguish registering in her eyes, there was a lot more to this story, and it was going to break his heart to hear it.

"No," he said, sipping his wine. "I'm trying to understand you. Your brother. The dynamic between the two of you and if there is some kind of weird cryptic message he's left you that we can't see."

She gripped the counter with both hands and lowered her head. "What happened to me has nothing to do with what's going on with Woodrow."

"Maybe not. But right now, I can't trust that you won't fly off the handle if I take you on base. I can't have that. We have no idea who we are dealing with and what they are doing. Until we have more information, we need things to be business as usual."

"Me showing up at Little Creek wouldn't be that."

"But it would be normal for you to be asking

questions. What I can't have is you behaving like you have been—"

She raised her hand. "Don't speak to me as if I were a child."

"I'm not," he said, pinching the bridge of his nose. "At least I don't feel like I am, but obviously the things I'm doing are triggering all sorts of negative responses. We need to find a way to make sure you don't do that on the base, especially when we don't know how big this leak is."

"You believe me? You believe that my brother didn't disappear on his own volition?"

"I believe that something doesn't add up, and I want to find out what." He stretched out his arm, taking her chin between his thumb and forefinger. "I promise I will be as honest with you as I can without doing something that will cause me to get court-martialed. But I need the same from you."

"I'm not keeping anything else from you, but I'm not going to discuss my marriage or what happened. It's not important. I'll keep my temper in check, and I'll work on my defiance issues." She curled her fingers around his wrist and tugged his hand away from her face. "But you have to stop doing things like that. I know you think you're being kind and gentle, but I struggled with having my personal space invaded when I was a kid, and it got worse when I married a monster."

"What the hell did he do to you?"

"It would be easier and take less time to tell you what he didn't do to me," she said, tucking her long dark hair behind her ears. "Crash wherever you want, but I'll warn you, I sleep with a gun, so I wouldn't go and startle me in the middle of the night."

He opened his mouth, but she shushed him by cupping his face with her palm. "I know my husband can't reach out from the dead and hurt me, but his family has made it clear they think I should be in jail, and while I haven't heard from them in over a year, his father broke into my house and threatened me."

"Shit. I'm sorry," he said, dropping his hands to his sides. "That is quite insensitive of me."

"One of the reasons this is so hard for me is that about a year into my marriage, I found a dose of courage and I asked for help from the doctor I was seeing on the base. I thought he was going to help me, only that night, my husband came home and broke two of my ribs and split my lip open. I don't trust the breeding ground that is the military."

Fuck. Her story was beyond complex. "And your brother? Do you trust him?"

"Yes and no," she said. "I trust that he's a good person and that he's nothing like Conrad. But I don't trust what the Navy might have turned him into." She waggled her finger. "That said, he was scared and worried for his safety. Something I can relate to."

"Fair enough."

"The couch is a pullout, and there are linens in the bathroom. And please, either text me or yell to me that you're coming upstairs. I wasn't kidding about the gun."

"Just remember you can't take it on base," he said, watching her jog up the stairs. He snagged his tablet and shot off a message to Tex. There had to be a lot more he could find on Olympia, her late husband, and his asshole family.

CHAPTER 5

Olympia stiffened her spine and breathed deeply and slowly. She hadn't been on a military base since she made herself go to her brother's graduation from the Naval Academy. It had only been about a year since Conrad had died, and her emotions had been so raw, but she owed it to her brother, and to her parents, to attend after everything she'd put them through.

"Is it okay if I put my hand on your back?" Landon whispered as they walked up the sidewalk toward the building her brother worked in.

"Yes." Oh boy. First, she wasn't used to men actually listening to her ridiculous demands. Her therapist had told her many times to stop using them as a way to make people dislike her and leave her alone, but it had become the only way she knew to protect herself from being hurt. The few relationships she'd had since Conrad were with decent, kind men who would never hit her, but she just couldn't allow herself to trust her own judgment long term.

Much less be happy for five minutes.

His hand felt comforting and strong as he guided her up the steps. "How are you holding up?"

"I'm fine."

He pulled open the door and immediately snapped to attention. "Commander Callahan. Commander Henry," Landon said.

"At ease, Lieutenant," one of the men said.

She leaned closer to Landon, slipping her arm around his waist, which caught her a sideways glance, but she ignored it as he didn't really seem to care all that much because he squeezed her hip.

"Good day," the other man said as he tucked something under his arm and strolled off down the street.

"Have a good day, Lieutenant," the other man said.

"Will do, Commander," Landon said as he nudged her forward.

"Who was that?" she asked as she stepped into the air conditioning. "Which one was Callahan?"

Landon glanced over his shoulder and pulled the

door closed. "The one who walked away first. Why?"

"I wanted to know who each commander was. Shouldn't we be checking into them?"

Landon did a double take, as if to make sure everyone was out of earshot. "You need to trust me and let me and my people do what we're good at."

"You don't make it easy for me to keep all my issues in check."

"But you're doing a good job."

"Right. Because I'm really thinking that all you're good at is killing and lying and not necessarily in that order."

"I suck at lying." He winked.

A female officer strolled down the hallway. "Lieutenant," the woman said.

"Emily," Landon said. "I'd like you to meet Olympia."

Emily's jaw slacked open. She glanced nervously around the room. "I've heard a lot of good things about you from your brother," Emily said. "But I don't think you should be here."

"Why is that?" Landon asked.

Emily leaned in. "You've heard what they are saying about Woodrow," she whispered. "And the investigation is heating up. Quinn is in the office today, going through everything. She's turned the office upside down."

"She's also here to meet with Olympia."

"Oh," Emily said. "For the record, I don't believe a word of what they are saying."

"Do you have a theory? Because someone did it." Landon held up his hand. "And I'm not implying it was you."

"I don't have an opinion. Excuse me." Emily scurried off and disappeared behind a door.

"Woodrow has a crush on her?" Olympia struggled with that concept. While Emily was pretty enough, her personality, at least what Olympia had seen so far, didn't fit into Woodrow's type.

"She's not normally that standoffish. But I bet Quinn ruffled her feathers. And she's taking a lot of heat since she's basically now responsible for your brother's job," Landon said as he guided her through a long corridor, passing by a few offices until they rounded a corner and stepped into a conference room.

A woman wearing a female naval officer's dress whites sat at the very far end of the room. She had a pair of black-rimmed reading glasses perched on the tip of her nose. Her red hair was pulled back into a tight bun low at the nape of her neck.

"Well, look at what the cat dragged in." The woman stood, smoothing down her perfectly pressed uniform, then glided across the floor as if she were an actress on the red carpet.

"Quinn." Landon, dressed in his sailor fatigues, kissed Quinn's cheek. "Thanks for taking this meeting."

"You didn't give me much of a choice." Quinn turned her gaze and looked Olympia up and down.

Olympia swallowed.

Quinn stretched out her arm. "I don't mean to be rude right off the bat, but I hope you won't make me regret this."

"I apologize for my outburst the last time we spoke," Olympia said.

"I appreciate that." Quinn looked younger than Olympia thought she would be, and her eyes were greener than an emerald. "I'm doing this as a personal favor to Landon and his team."

To Olympia, that meant this would be a total waste of her fucking time. Quinn, and her snakelike mesmerizing eyes, didn't care about her or her brother, and she really didn't care about finding the truth. If she did, she wouldn't take this kind of attitude.

Olympia bit down on her tongue. If she went off at the mouth, Landon might not help her anymore, and he was all she had. And so far, he'd done everything she'd requested. Most people wouldn't do that.

"Please, make yourself comfortable," Quinn said.

Landon pulled back a chair, offering it Olympia, and she gladly took it, rubbing her hands up and down her thighs. She'd called Quinn a few times, leaving nasty messages on her machine, calling her names that she probably didn't deserve.

Frustration wasn't an excuse for Olympia's outburst. Nor was her overcompensation for not having a voice most of her life and then having it beat out of her during her marriage. Being an angry person had worked for her for a couple of years after her husband died. It kept people away while she learned to live with the very real fact that she'd taken another's life. Didn't matter that Conrad was a horrible human being, she wasn't God.

But now all being in full rage did was make her look like a bitter woman.

"Landon and his friends have uncovered some interesting things, but so far, nothing that makes your brother look good," Quinn said.

"I understand that." Olympia crossed her ankles, making sure her shoulder blades pulled her posture taller. Resting her hands in her lap, she picked at her thumbnail, hoping it would keep her from rattling her knee. "I can see how it looks bad."

"But someone broke into his place and took his bank records, which is weird," Landon said. "Not to mention someone put spyware on his computer."

Quinn set her pen down on the table and clasped her fingers. "And where is this computer now?"

"With Tex," Landon said.

"You've got to be fucking kidding me." Quinn pounded her knuckles on the wood top twice. "That's evidence in an active case that you just compromised."

"Tex knows the drill, and he'll give you everything, but I couldn't risk whoever installed the predatory program to get a lock on the location, which happened to be my condo building."

Quinn laughed. "All you had to do was disconnect it and give it to me, but no, you had to send it to Tex, and that means, no matter how good Tex is, whatever he finds is compromised and potentially useless in a case against Woodrow."

"That is if, and only if, he really went AWOL,

because you have to admit, there are some red flags and large holes in that theory." Landon leaned back and folded his arms.

Quinn pursed her lips. "It's not a theory. Lieutenant Woodrow Anderson *is* AWOL. That is a fact."

"But what isn't fact is why or how he came to be AWOL. And some of things I brought this morning, you have to admit give pause."

Olympia glanced between Landon and Quinn, not really understanding the dynamic between the two, but Olympia did have newfound respect for Landon. Of course, there was that little voice in the back of her mind that whispered: *Landon is lying. He's playing you. This is all a game. Don't trust him. He's no different than any other military man.*

He's no different than Conrad.

She shoved that thought back. Of course Landon was different. He'd already proven that. Besides, she'd never be in a relationship with the man, so she'd never find out if he was a good man outside of being loyal to his country.

There was a difference.

"There are a lot of things in this case that make me wonder a plethora of things." Quinn cleared her throat and stared at Olympia with daggers shooting from her emerald eyes. "Like why did Woodrow put money in an offshore account for his sister and try to hide it?"

"I have a theory on that." Olympia thought long and hard about whether to add this to the mix, but decided she really had nothing to lose. "When I got married, my husband forged the paperwork to legally change my name. That's something I would never do. I don't like to conform to tradition."

"I'm bored," Quinn said. "This doesn't matter to me."

Olympia inhaled sharply, swallowing her breath, along with her sharp tongue. "But it matters to my brother and how his mind worked and the way he did things."

"Weren't you and Woodrow estranged for a few years?" Quinn asked.

Landon reached under the table and squeezed her knee.

Normally, she'd elbow him in the ribs, but honestly, his gentle reminder to keep cool actually calmed her nerves. That was a new sensation, and she didn't want to welcome it, but she needed to.

"I left home one day after I turned eighteen. I married my husband the day after I graduated from high school. My family stopped talking to me before

I got my diploma. Or maybe I stopped talking to them. That was until I was arrested for killing my husband." That was the first time she'd gotten through that story without a few sarcastic remarks that made her out to be Hannibal Lector's twin sister.

"And that was when you were twenty. So, five years ago?" Quinn asked. "So, when did you change your name back to Anderson?"

"The second they released me and I was cleared, but what's important here is all the things my husband put in my name that I had no idea about until after he died. And they kept popping up, including a couple offshore bank accounts that he was trying to hide."

"Wait a minute," Landon said. "You didn't tell me that last night."

She nodded. "My trust level isn't very high, but I also wasn't exactly thinking straight. Now that my brain has had some time to process all of this, I can't help but think this is a clue."

"How so?" Quinn asked.

"When we found the accounts, my husband's estate had already been settled, and I gave everything back to his horrible family."

"Everything?" Quinn opened a file and ran a

finger down a sheet of paper. "I read here your late husband was worth a few million."

"Fifteen and some change," Olympia said. "But I didn't want any of his money. My brother and my parents thought I should take it for what he'd done to me."

"I'd have to agree with them," Landon said under his breath.

"Let's stick with how you believe this is some kind of clue as to where your brother is," Quinn said.

"Not where, but that he's still alive and that, first, the money isn't his, and two, he wanted me to come here to cause trouble." Olympia's heartbeat raced. Her chest rose up and down while she could no longer fill her lungs. She grabbed Landon's hand under the table. "He knew I wouldn't take the money and run. He knew I'd let my temper get the better of me, and he knew I'd come looking for Landon."

"How did he know all that?" Quinn said.

"Because he set it up that way," Landon said, shaking his head.

"I'm still not sure I'm following, much less buying this, but if this were true, where did the money come from?" Quinn asked.

"Seriously, Quinn? You know exactly where it came from. The rumors are true," Landon said.

"Excuse me?" Olympia shoved his hand aside.

"I don't mean that your brother actually sold top secret plans." He folded his arms on the table. "Quinn, do you remember Keanu's Squad Two's mission last week?"

"We can't talk about that here," she said behind tight lips.

"Not the details, but remember the anonymous tip?" Landon said. "What if Woodrow took the money from whoever hired him to give bad intel, but then informed our team about a potential deadly ambush?"

Quinn stood, gathering her things. "That's a pretty tall tale with nothing concrete to go on, and I like my theory better."

"And what's that?" Landon asked.

"That Woodrow took money to sell information, and he didn't do what he was supposed to and instead took the money and ran."

"Makes perfect sense." Olympia bolted from her seat, blocking Quinn's path to the door. "Only you're not taking into consideration the fact he didn't take the money. He gave it to me."

"Then you must be in on it," Quinn said with an indignant smile plastered across her freckled face.

"If that were the case, I wouldn't be here letting

you people rip apart the worst parts of my life. I'd be in Aruba sipping on a tropical drink with a stupid umbrella popping out of the top and living the dream."

Quinn cocked her head as she stepped to the side. "Landon, I expect to kept in the loop with Tex and whatever he uncovers with Woodrow's laptop."

"Tex said he'd copy you on everything," Landon said.

Olympia gripped one of the chairs for support. The room spun as she struggled for breath. She opened her mouth, but no words came out.

"If either of you think of anything useful, please give me a call." Quinn pulled open the door. "For the record, I have a hard time believing Woodrow would sell anyone top secret information, but someone in this office was supposed to, and now I'm hearing rumors it's about to happen again."

"So, you know it can't be my brother," Olympia said.

"Actually, I don't. He could be pulling the strings." Quinn held up her hand. "But I will assure you that I'm keeping an open mind, which means that everything you tell me or show me, I'm going to look into, but, and just so you know how I operate, I will always argue and do what I can to poke holes in it, because that's the only way I'm going to find the truth. Now, if you will excuse me, I have work to do."

Olympia stood in the doorway with her jaw slacked open. She wasn't sure what to make of that encounter. Quinn had treated her as if Olympia were the enemy, and yet it felt as though Quinn might actually believe the direction Olympia was going.

"Interesting theory," Landon said, stepping in front of her.

She stared into his warm chocolate eyes. "If I'm right, it means my brother is alive."

"And you had always thought he was dead?"

She wiped a tear from her cheek. "He wouldn't go AWOL, not without a reason. So until that formed in my head, him being murdered was the only thing that made sense."

He ran his hands up and down her forearms. "Any other theories you want to share?"

"Not yet. But now that I've checked my attitude at the door, maybe I can be of better use."

Landon nodded. "It's quitting time. Why don't we head back to my place and mull everything over?"

"Sounds like a plan."

* * *

Landon punched the pillow and rolled to the side. The screen on his cell blinked three in the morning. He'd dozed off for maybe two hours. He was hoping he'd be able to fall asleep for a few more, but all he could think about was Olympia.

He should have insisted on sleeping on her sofa again. It didn't make him feel any better that security cameras had been installed, covering all entrance points. And he especially didn't like she slept with a gun. He could understand why, but he didn't like it.

He propped himself up and stared out the window. The moon shined bright in the dark sky, casting a white glow across the calm sea. He could hear the ocean waves gently lapping at the beach. The salty air carried across the slight breeze into his room. He'd always loved the water, and living near it soothed his broken heart.

But now his heart ached for something he couldn't have.

Something he didn't want.

And for sure, something Olympia couldn't give.

His phone rang, startling him. He reached across the bed and snagged it off the nightstand.

"Olympia? Is everything okay?"

"No," she said so softly it was barely audible. "I think I hear someone outside."

"Stay on the line." He jumped from the bed, hiking up a pair of jeans. He raced across the room and flipped open his laptop, clicking on the security cameras links. "Nothing looks out of the ordinary on the security cameras, but let me check the perimeter."

"I'll go with you."

"Please, stay inside. I'll put in my AirPods, and we can stay connected that way."

"Okay," she said.

He slipped his feet into a pair of flip-flops and snuck out into the warm night using only the light from the stars. The only real access points to her house were the front porch that overlooked the ocean and the sliders that opened up to a shared backyard. He started there and didn't like the fact that the fence wasn't latched.

Didn't mean anything, and it could have been kids from down at the end of the building. They were always forgetting to secure the fence.

"Where are you?" she whispered.

"Backyard," he responded, scanning the grassy patch. The motion tension should have kicked the spotlight on by now. He noticed what looked like a piece of paper tucked under the mat. He bent over and picked it up. The words: *Olympia Anderson* were written on the front facing of an envelope.

"Let me in," he whispered.

"On it."

He didn't have to wait more than a few seconds before she was standing in front of him wearing nothing but boxers and a flimsy spaghetti strap top, obviously with no bra underneath. He blinked. "Did you look at the cameras before you called me?"

"I did," she said. "And I was watching just now, but you didn't show up."

"Fuck," he mumbled. "This was left for you."

She reached for it, but he snapped it away.

"We can't have any more fingerprints on it." Carefully, he set it on the table. "Hey Siri, call Quinn Thatcher," he said.

"This better be fucking good." Quinn answered on the second ring. She sounded like she had a frog in her throat.

"Someone tampered with my security cameras at

Olympia's condo, making themselves invisible while leaving her a note."

"What does the note say?" Quinn asked.

"It's sealed in an envelope. My fingerprints are on it."

"Take a fork to hold it down and use a knife to open it. Do your best to tug it out without putting more prints on it and read it to me," Quinn said.

Olympia held the fork steady while Landon ripped open the paper and successfully unfolded the note.

"You have some things that belong to me, and I want them back. You have until the end of the week to get them to me. You can wire the money to the account listed below. And the defense plans your brother stole, you'll be given instructions on how to get them to me. If you fail, your brother dies."

The fork spun and dropped to the floor.

Olympia covered her mouth and gasped. "He's really still alive."

Landon didn't have it in his heart to tell her that it could all be a lie to get her to do exactly what the bad guy wanted.

"I'll be over in twenty," Quinn said. "Don't call the locals. Got it?"

"Loud and clear," Landon said as he ended the

call. "We need to find and get into that safety deposit box."

"What if the key belongs to something else?" Olympia chewed on her thumbnail.

"Okay. Elaborate." He planted his hands on his hips, doing his best to remain calm. She'd been through a lot, and she didn't trust easily.

"You're going to have to let me get through this my way—"

"Just start talking because I'm listening."

She nodded. "Remember I said you were in the office the last time I spoke with Woodrow."

"Yes." Landon had no idea what this had to do with a key, but he had gotten to know her well enough to know there was a method to her madness.

"Well, I was thinking about that day because I actually spoke to him twice. The first time, he mentioned you might be coming into the office and he would have to go if that were the case. But he cut me off when someone else came in."

"Who?"

"He whispered it really softly, but I'm pretty sure he said Callahan right before he hung up."

Landon rubbed his forehead. "Okay. So, there is chatter about the base that on more than one occasion Woodrow might have butted heads with Callahan, but Callahan is well-liked and respected. He has a long-standing career in the Navy."

"And my husband was a major in the Marines. No one wanted to believe he would basically hold me captive in my own home and repeatedly beat the shit out of me, leaving behind permanent scars." She lifted up her shirt, showing off a burn that took up half her stomach, stretching to the sides and around to her back.

"Jesus." He reached out and traced the veiny pink skin with his fingers. "Looks like a grease burn."

"Smart man. The best part about this one is he had everyone believing I was so distraught after my miscarriage that I might have hurt myself on purpose."

A guttural moan filled his throat. "Fucking bastard."

"Tell me about it," she said. "Now excuse me if I don't give a shit if anyone respects him. You have no idea if he has a dark side. Hell, my gut says you're one of the very rare few good men. The kind of man my brother is, and I say that because everything Woodrow did led me to you. But you could still be a monster behind closed doors."

"We all have our demons," he mumbled. "But I'm no monster." His chest tightened, and it became increasingly difficult to breathe. The images bombarded his mind, filling his soul with death and pain. He squeezed his eyes shut, rubbing hard, as if that would erase the horrific memory of the night he found his wife and child dead. "Your point is well heard. Can we get back to the key?"

Her hand came down on his bare shoulder. Her warm fingers gently massaged his tense muscle. "Are you okay?"

"I get migraines, and one is coming on." He shouldn't lie, but he wasn't going to fall apart in front of her either. He'd hold off his sheer panic followed by an hour of crying until after this was over. He'd done it before; he'd be able to do it again, even if he had to do it for a week. "The key. What were you thinking about the key?"

"Here, sit down." She guided him to the chair in the kitchen and rubbed the back of his neck, up the sides of his head and along his temples.

If it didn't feel so fucking good, he'd tell her to stop.

"So, Woodrow called me back. I asked him about what happened, and he said he couldn't talk about it. That he could see you heading toward his office."

Landon rotated his head. "What? If he was in his

office, he couldn't see me unless he was wandering the halls."

"No. He said he could see you walking up the street."

"That doesn't make sense, unless he was outside."

"But I could hear people in the background. And then he got weird."

"Weird how?"

"He started talking about how I'd like you and that if I ever came to visit, he wanted to introduce us, which started an argument on my end. That's when he brought up the key."

Landon reached behind him and grabbed her wrist. "The key we found behind the toilet?"

"I'm thinking yes," she said. "But it doesn't go to a safety deposit box, but a home safe."

Without really thinking about what he was doing, he tugged her to his lap, wrapping his arms around her waist. "Why would he bring up a key during that conversation?"

"He was teasing me because when we were kids, I used to have to hide my diary from him in a safe, and he always found my key. He said I couldn't hide anything to save my ass."

"I'm still not following why this has anything to do with me," Landon said.

"Woodrow thought you reminded him of my boyfriend before I ended up running off with the devil."

"And do I?" he asked.

She laughed. "No. Not at all. Which is why I don't think I really thought anything of it, but he said you were the kind of man I'd want to tell my diary about and then lock it up in my safe so he couldn't embarrass me. After he said that, he started whispering again and then said you came in and he had to go."

"Okay, stupid question since we didn't find a safe in your brother's place; do you have one?"

She nodded. "I do. It's upstairs in my bedroom."

"Of course you do." He tilted his head, holding her gaze.

Her lips parted, and he simply couldn't resist the need to feel them rub against his in a tender kiss. Thankfully, she didn't pull away.

Or slap him.

She didn't deepen the kiss, but she participated, and that was something totally unexpected. As was the sudden floating of butterflies in his gut.

He pulled back. "We should go get it." He stood, still holding her by the hips.

"Aren't you going to ask me if I'm missing my key?"

He cocked his head. “And when did you check on that?”

“Right after I called you.” She took a step back and lowered her gaze. “You really should learn to button your pants.”

He groaned.

CHAPTER 6

Olympia held her breath while she watched Landon carefully insert the key into her safe. "I still can't figure out how he got the key and hid it." She touched her lips, wondering why she felt so comfortable and confident in Landon's arms. She kept trying to tell herself to push him away, but her brother's voice whispering that she'd like Landon echoed in her mind.

Her brother had always known her better than anyone.

"Either him or someone else is watching you." Landon had nerves of steel. Throughout all of this, he'd remained calm and he'd been her rock, but she would need him to clarify his statement about how everyone had demons.

"I want that digital footage." Quinn hovered over Landon like a praying mantis.

"I told you I'd make sure you got a copy of everything." Landon turned the key and lifted open the safe. "Holy shit." He pulled out five folders with *top secret* typed in bold face letters across the top.

"How the fuck did you get these?" Quinn practically knocked Landon over as she snatched them up.

"I have no idea how they got there. I swear," Olympia said with a shaky voice.

Landon wrapped an arm around her, pulling her tight against his body. "You know she didn't have anything to do with those files."

"I don't know that," Quinn said, stuffing them into her bag. "What you don't know is that these went missing at the same time Woodrow did. However, the powers that be didn't want it known."

Olympia turned and faced Landon. "Whoever has my brother didn't get him until after I got here."

"Or someone is helping him," Quinn said. "It just seems like Woodrow has always been one step ahead of both me and whoever he's buying and selling for."

"He's not selling though," Landon said. "Don't you see that?"

"I'm keeping all my options open." Quinn let out a long breath. "Is there anything else in there?"

Olympia pulled the safe across the table and glanced inside. Her heart hurt as she stared at one of the images of her badly beaten face. There were a dozen more like it stacked underneath along with copies of her hospital records, all saying ridiculous things like she fell rollerblading. Or they'd gone horseback riding, and hers had gotten a little out of control. Conrad had come up with a million reasons why she was always black and blue.

But it was the reason he gave for how she lost the baby that made her want to crawl under a rock and die.

She pressed her hand against her flat stomach. She'd only been five months, but she'd felt life growing in her belly.

Landon closed the lid. "Just her personal belongings." He laced his fingers through hers.

"I need you both in my office at ten sharp. Got it?" Quinn tossed her bag over her shoulder.

"Quinn, that won't be a problem, but I'll be bringing my team, and you will be briefing them, and we will be developing a plan to find and rescue Woodrow."

"Or capture. But yeah. I'm on board with that. Now if you will excuse me. I'm a total bitch without my coffee and my shower."

Olympia not only waited until Quinn was out the door, but she counted to ten before opening her mouth. "Is she always so nasty?"

"She's under a lot of pressure. Woodrow's disappearance with all the rumors spreading and now finding those files, it not only puts her in an awkward position, but it could but sailors' lives at risk."

"Well, I don't want that." Taking a risk she hadn't done in a long time, she leaned into his strong frame and wrapped her arms around him. "For the record, I'm not as angry as I come off. I've had two relationships since I became a widow, and both weren't very good, so I use what happened to keep people away. It works for me. And truthfully, I still sometimes struggle with things like nightmares and panic, but I'm much better."

"I understand."

She tilted her head. "I take it that's what you meant by everyone has their own demons?"

He fanned her face. "I'm so sorry for what your husband did to you, and it breaks my heart you have to live with taking a human life. I do know what that does to a person, even when it's kill or be killed." He wiped the tears burning a trail down her cheeks. "I also know loss and losing a child; even an unborn one is devastating."

She gasped as he kissed her temple. Most people who heard about her loss would either tell her what a blessing it had been because who would want to raise Conrad's child. Or they'd say something about at least she knew she could get pregnant and someday she'd have a child with a good man.

No one ever acknowledged the fact that she lost the idea of a person that she'd already fallen in love with.

Except for her parents. Woodrow.

And now Landon.

"Listen. I have this big bathtub with jets and everything. Why don't you come over and take advantage of it. I'll cook us a big breakfast, and then we can drive to the base together."

"That sounds wonderful. Thank you."

He kissed her, slipping his hot tongue between her lips, finding every crevice. She wrapped hers around his, matching his tender desire. While it was a passionate embrace, he didn't bring it to the next level. Instead, he held her for a long moment, stroking her hair, comforting her.

Letting herself go, she shuddered against his touch. She wasn't sure she'd ever felt this safe and protected in a man's arms. She splayed her hand across the center of his chest. "Just let me go get some of my things."

He tilted her chin with his thumb and his forefinger. "I don't know what is happening here between us, but when this is over, I'd like to take you out on a date."

She chuckled. "When we find my brother, I have a feeling he's going to demand it."

* * *

Landon sat on the edge of his bed, holding the very last picture he'd taken of Linda and Ryker before Linda changed the course of his life forever.

Only, Olympia made him question his ability to keep his mind, body, and soul firmly planted in the past while existing in the present without having any future. Blaming himself for what happened to Ryker he used like a badge of honor. Much like what he suspected Olympia did with what happened with her husband. It felt to him as though she blamed herself for not seeing what a monster he'd been from the beginning.

Just like how he believed he should have seen that Linda wasn't doing better at all.

He hated crying. Resented the fuck out of it. He tried to avoid it at all costs, but sometimes, there was no stopping the tears, like right now.

But he wasn't sure if the waterworks was for his loss.

Or what Olympia had been through.

Both equally horrific in their own right.

He kept pictures of his family in part to torture himself. Olympia kept images of her abuse to remind herself that oftentimes people lived behind a lie.

Landon had created this world for himself that didn't include his family. It wasn't a lie, but it wasn't reality either. And according to Abe, Alabama, Wyatt, and Clover, Landon created a narrative that not only held him responsible for things he had no control over, but kept him from moving forward.

He now knew they were absolutely correct. Only, he wasn't sure how to move past it. He didn't know how to create a new narrative, and he figured Olympia didn't either.

But their kiss was real.

And so was their connection and passion. Neither one could deny that, even though they both tried.

He swiped at his face, willing the tears to stop.

"Landon?"

He jumped at the sound of Olympia's voice, dropping the photograph to the floor by his feet.

"Sorry," she said as she bent over and snagged the picture.

He tried to take it from her, but she turned her body and took a step away. "What is this? You have a family? A child?"

"Not anymore." He pushed himself fully onto the bed, fluffing the pillow. The tears dried up, but his heart still squeezed tight, bleeding out in his chest cavity. For the first time since Linda took both her own life, and the life of their baby, he found himself not wanting to close himself off from the story that made him the man he was today. He crossed his ankles and clasped his fingers behind his head. "How was your bath?" He tried not to stare too hard. All she wore was a towel wrapped on her head, a pair of his shorts, and an oversized tank top with no bra, showing off the swell of her perfectly round breasts that he guessed to be about a B cup. Not that it mattered, but it would be the perfect fit in his palm.

He blinked. He really needed to stop thinking that way. It wasn't very becoming of a grieving sailor, much less a man helping a woman deal with a shit ton of crap.

"What does that mean?"

"They are both dead," he said, thick emotion clogging his throat. He tried to swallow, but his muscles wouldn't complete the task. The problem was he couldn't tell if it was because he had one foot in the past or because he was letting his heart taste a sliver of what opening up to another person again could be like.

The pull to Olympia ever since she'd shown up at his doorstep asking for a stupid plunger had been something he never thought he'd be capable of. The desire to get to know a woman and allow her into his soul he thought had died when he buried Ryker.

He'd failed his wife.

Worse. He failed as a father.

"I'm sorry." Olympia held the picture between her dainty fingers. She eased her ass to the side of the bed and rested her free hand on his knee. "What happened?"

"It's an ugly and depressing story."

"After I was finally cleared and my husband's death was ruled self-defense, thanks to the insanity of me keeping all those pictures and records of what he did to me, I couldn't stand the way people stared at me. They either pitied me, or they called me a murderer. I couldn't leave my parents' house. I was safe and no one was beating me anymore, but I was still living in a prison. That's when I quit my job and moved to the middle of nowhere in the Adirondacks. Close enough to civilization that I could deal with my clients, but far enough away that I didn't have to deal with people, especially those who knew who I was."

He took her hand, running his fingers over her soft skin. "Anyone ever tell you that you take forever to tell a story?"

She let out a nervous laugh. "My husband hated that about me. It caused a few bruises."

Landon inhaled sharply. "I think it's endearing. Please continue." He liked the sound of her voice, and whatever she wanted to share, he'd soak it in as if he were a sponge, even if he had no idea where she was going with her tale. Honestly, he couldn't care less. Just being with her made things better.

"The only person I ever talked to about what happened outside of my family was my therapist, who, to this day tells me, keeping one foot solidly planted in the past is a surefire way to make sure that not only will history not repeat itself, but neither will the opportunity to live again. I'm starting to believe she's right. I guess I'm taking a long time to say my story is brutal and dirty. If anyone understands ugly, it's me."

He hated to admit it, but she had a point. "Is this a misery loves company kind of thing?"

"Maybe it's time to put an end to the misery. I'm tired of being the angry bitch who murdered her husband in self-defense. It's a heavy burden to carry. This might sound crazy, but some of that has been lifted with you seeing those pictures."

"Why do you think that is?"

"Because you don't pity me. You're not judging me. And you're not telling me that I might have done something to set him off."

"Bite your fucking tongue," he said behind gritted teeth. "Anyone who would blame the victim is a moron."

"Well, there are a lot of morons out there then." She handed him the picture. "Most men would have sent me packing the second I broke into your house, but not you. You're a good man, and everyone can see that, but you're not whole, and that shows too."

"Aren't you insightful," he said, holding her hand in the air while he examined her long manicured fingers as his mind digested her words. His heart didn't need to because it begged him to let her in. The last time he'd told a woman about Linda and Ryker, it had been Clover, and that had only been to help her understand her future husband's mindset over the loss of his child. It had been told in an emotionless moment with the intent to help a friend and to see if he had it in him to move forward.

He hadn't.

At least not at that moment in time.

"I'm a master at hiding behind whatever mask I want to put on any given day. You seem to only have one, but you wear it well." She leaned forward and kissed his cheek. "Tell me about your family."

He moved over, making room for her to lay her head in his lap. Yanking the towel off her head, he stared down at her while he stroked her long hair and traced a couple of faint scars that snaked from her ear to under her chin.

"Would it help if I asked you questions?"

He chuckled. "It might because I'm a little distracted right now."

She arched a brow. "I'm going to take that as a compliment."

"Good. Because you should. Women don't affect me like you do."

"What does that mean?" She narrowed her eyes.

He blew out a long breath and held up the picture of Linda and Ryker. "I've always thought when they died, I died with them, but you make me feel alive like I haven't in years."

"The feeling is mutual, but I'm not going to let you use that to get out of telling me what happened. How long ago did they pass away?"

"Almost six years," he admitted. "Linda and I got married while I was still in the Naval Academy. I was twenty, she was nineteen. Her mother tried to warn me what I was getting into, but I didn't listen."

"What do you mean?"

"Linda was bipolar, and when she was on her meds, she was fine. But when she went off them, like she had to when she was pregnant, things could get scary. Her mental illness was extreme, and in the year we dated, I didn't see it, but looking back, I should have."

"Oh, do I know the should-have train. I'm actually the conductor. Conrad was such a charmer, or should I say, gaslighter."

"In a way, so was Linda. But she used emotional blackmail. Only, off her meds, she didn't have the mental capacity to know that's what she was doing. Of course, all this is a grown man looking back. I didn't know any of this when I was living it."

"The first time Conrad hit me, I wanted to leave, but he snowed me into believing it would never happen again. Eventually, he had me thinking that it was my fault he used his fists."

"That's the way abuse works. No one ever understands how hard it is for the victim to leave." Landon had seen it all too many times. "The Linda I fell in love with was kind and sweet and the happiest person I've ever known. Everyone thought we were nuts for getting married so quickly and then for having a baby right away, but we were happy. Or so I thought."

"When did she go off her medication?" Olympia asked.

"Sometime before the wedding. Looking back, I can see some of the manic behavior, but I thought that was just excitement. And then all the emotional mood swings, well, I chalked it up to being the bride of a man still in the academy. My schedule was brutal, and right after graduation it was right into my first deployment and subsequent SEAL training. I didn't see her slipping into a major depression during the end the pregnancy, and it got worse after Ryker was born."

Olympia closed her eyes. Her chest rose as she took in long breath. A tear squeezed out of the corner of her eye.

He reached out and wiped it away. "By the time Ryker was a few months old, Linda wouldn't get out of bed, and when she did, she would say and do things that scared the shit out of me. I called her mom, and we were able to talk Linda into going back on her meds and seeing a therapist. I was able to take some time off and was willing to do whatever it took to make my family whole." He continued to watch Olympia breathe, which seemed to become a bit of a struggle. Her lips quivered as she released the air from her lungs.

"Hey." He tugged at a strand of her hair. "Come here." He pulled her into his arms, cradling her head on his shoulder.

She pressed her lips against his chest, letting them linger for a long moment. Her fingers danced up and down his arm.

"I thought she was taking her meds, and she really seemed to be doing better, but it was all an act."

"Oh, God," Olympia whispered, wrapping her leg over his, holding him so tight he could barely breathe.

Instead of peeling her off him, he eased himself lower on the bed and ran his hands up and down her back.

"I expected to hear something like they were killed in a car crash when you were deployed and you felt guilty. Or maybe hit by a drunk driver. A freak accident. But if what is playing out in my mind is what happened, I wasn't prepared to hear it."

"Nor was I prepared to see what that bastard did to you. If he wasn't already dead, I'd murder him myself."

"That would land you in jail, and you wouldn't be able claim self-defense."

He burst out laughing. It was funny, and it was totally inappropriate, but in the moment, it was sorely needed.

She slapped his chest. "My comic relief came too soon. We both need you to finish the story."

He took her hand and kissed the palm. She was right. "I've never told anyone this story that I wanted to start a relationship with."

She jerked her head. "That's a big jump from knowing we're going to have sex to thinking I'm going to stick around to have it a tenth time."

"At least I know it will happen more than once." He rolled to his side, so he could gaze into her eyes. He needed her strength. "Linda promised me things were different. That she'd turned the corner, and I believed her, so I went back to work. A week later, I came home to find my wife and son dead, in our bed. She'd killed Ryker and then killed herself, and she had that picture in her hand."

Olympia pressed her mouth against his in a short, tender kiss.

He held her for a long moment, letting the tears flow freely, scorching a path down his cheeks. He wasn't really crying, but his body was purging all the guilt he held so close to his heart for the sole purpose of torturing his mind. He allowed his anguish to race through his bloodstream, poisoning every aspect of his life.

It was time to stop.

"We're quite a pair, aren't we," he whispered.

"Yes, we are," she said. "Crazy question, but did my brother know about Linda and your son?"

"I don't think so. I don't tell people, but I suppose it's possible."

"Well, it makes sense why he thought I would like you, because he knew we would relate to each other."

"One thing your brother did know about me," Landon said as he took her chin between his thumb and forefinger. "Is that I don't know how to sit on the sidelines. He set this up well."

"Only now he's being held captive because that note says they will kill him," she said with wide eyes.

"I'm going to do whatever it takes to make sure that doesn't happen." He brushed his mouth over hers slowly, tenderly, and methodically. He wanted her so badly, it hurt.

And it scared him.

Sex was a need.

Not a desire.

He hadn't felt passion since long before Linda died, and he never thought he'd ever feel it again, much less want it. But he found himself dreaming about romantic walks on the beach, wine on the patio, and waking up with her hair pooled over his chest.

"You're trembling." She flattened her hand against his stomach.

"So are you."

She tossed her leg over his thighs and straddled him. Her fingers toyed with the fabric of her shirt. "I don't want to scare you off, but I still have some residual side effects left over from being abused."

"That's understandable." He reached up, cupping the back of her neck and massaging gently. "We only have a couple of hours before we have to get to the base. We probably should take a nap."

"We can have both."

"I'm not going to say no, but I want you to feel safe and comfortable, and at any time, we can stop. I do get that no means exactly that." He rolled her shirt halfway up, showing off some of her scars. He leaned up and kissed them.

"Can we have a safe word?"

"We can have whatever you want," he said. "You're in control. You tell me what to do and how to do it."

She pressed her finger under his chin. "I have all the power?"

"I would never hurt you. I'll do whatever you need to show you that's true."

She bit down on her lower lip and arched her brow.

"What are you thinking?"

"I'll try to keep this explanation short." She lifted the flimsy T-shirt up over her head, exposing perfectly round breasts.

He groaned, holding on to her hips. He wouldn't touch until she told him it was okay. This would certainly prove to be a test in constraint.

"I'm listening."

"You're staring, but that's okay," she said with a smile. "The few times I've had sex since, well, you know, I have to be on top."

"One of my favorite positions."

"You're a guy. I think you'll take it any way you can get it."

"Good point," he said.

"But even then, I sometimes panic, and it all has to do with feeling out of control."

He stretched his arms out wide to the sides as if he were making a *T* in the bed. "I'll just lay here."

"You say that now, but it will be hard for you not to reach out and grab something unless you were tied up."

He opened his mouth and croaked. "You want to tie me up the very first time we have sex?"

"You'd have a safe word. I mean, I do understand consent." She winked.

Never in his life did he think he'd let a woman restrain him. Quite honestly, he never thought about doing it to a sexual partner. Just wasn't his thing. But if it made her feel comfortable and helped her get over her past so she could realize not all men were monsters, then so be it. "Okay, but if I say *Navy*, you have to stop whatever it is you're doing."

"All right."

"And I want warnings before you do things."

"Anything else?" She slipped from the bed and stood over him with her hands on her hips and nipples poking through her thick hair.

"I have a condom in the top drawer of my nightstand. We should probably use it."

"I'm on the pill and haven't had sex in over six months."

"About the same." He fisted the sheets. "We can go without, then."

"Now I just need to find something to tie you up with."

CHAPTER 7

Olympia finished securing Landon's wrists using bandanas he'd collected and used for when he took out the Harley. She stood at the end of the bed, admiring her work, noticing the excitement pressing against the zipper of his jeans.

"I should have taken off my pants first," he said with a thick, deep voice.

She crawled across the mattress, her fingers hovering over his body.

"Be careful. I'm not wearing any underwear."

What the fuck had she talked herself into? Her therapist had always told her that the best ways for her to work through her sexual issues were to first, be open—something she had never done until now. And second, share her wants, her desires, her needs.

Teach whoever became her partner how to please and love her the way she'd always dreamed of.

But she was afraid the second he climbed on top of her, she'd freak out and punch the poor man.

It happened once before.

It could happen again.

Carefully, she lifted the waistband of his pants and slipped her fingers between his bare warm skin and the cold zipper.

He hissed.

"Did I hurt you?"

His eyes fluttered closed. "Good Lord, no."

A full smile spread across her face, spreading her cheeks, making them hurt. Gently, she tugged at the metal. He pressed against her hand.

She held her breath and didn't move for a long moment. Her therapist always told her that the moment she turned on her fears and changed her narrative, her world would open up, and she'd be able to mend her broken soul.

This was her chance.

She blinked open her eyes and rolled his pants down over his hips, yanking them to his ankles where he kicked out of them, sending them across the room.

Shamelessly, she stared at him, studying every

twitch his muscles made. His tanned skin brightened as the morning sun peeked through the window.

"I feel naked and tied up," he said.

She wiggled out of her shorts.

"This is torture, you know that, right?"

"You have a safe word."

"And I have no desire to use it," he said with a raspy breath.

"Good. But you'll have to tell me if I'm doing this right."

"Excuse me?" He lifted his head off the bed.

"That didn't come out right." She sat on the bed between his legs and tucked her hair behind her ears. "I don't want to ruin this."

"You won't, so just say it."

"He always forced me to do this."

"Jesus," Landon mumbled. "You don't have to do. Not to be crude, but blowjobs, handjobs, they don't have to be part of sex. I don't need them. It's okay if you don't want to."

She reached out and squeezed his thighs, digging in with her fingers, moving up and down. With each stroke, she moved closer to the prize. "Before him, I'd done it a couple of times and I remembered liking it. I want to like it again. I want to like all of this again, but I have to be in control. Will you let me?"

"Oh, fuck yeah." He tossed his head back on the pillow "But just know I'm not into biting or hand and fingers going places they don't belong."

"Neither am I," she said.

She continued to move her hands over his body, letting her hair glide across his hardness, enjoying his soft moans and occasional tug at his constraints. Gliding her finger over his length, she inhaled sharply. There was an intense contrast between his silky skin and the firmness she held in her hands.

He raised his knees, digging his ankles into the bed when she took her tongue and rolled it over the tip.

A rush of heat raced through her system. Her nipples tightened and throbbed. Her body responded to him in ways she only dreamed for the last few years.

Greedily, she took him into her mouth, letting her hands lead the way.

"Olympia?"

She paused, glancing up at him. Her heart hammering in her chest that perhaps he didn't like what she was doing.

"Will you move your hair so I can watch you?"

Her eyes widened, and a bolt of heat spread between her legs like a wild fire.

Quickly, she piled her hair on top of her head, slipping her hair tie from her wrist around it in a messy bun.

"Thank you," he said between ragged breaths.

She enjoyed the way he felt in her mouth, and surprisingly, she loved glancing up at him every once in a while, catching his smoldering gaze as he admired the pleasure she brought to his body.

"Sort of Navy," he said behind a guttural moan.

"Sort of?"

"Well, I don't want to stop, but I need you to stop that, or this will end in about sixty seconds because I won't be able to control myself anymore."

She sat up a little taller and smiled proudly.

"Unless that's what you want, because you can have whatever your heart desires."

"Right now, all I want is this." She settled on top of him, only taking the tip inside her while she leaned over, letting her breast dangle in front of his mouth about an inch away.

He licked his lips, lifting his head off the pillow. "May I?"

"Please." She arched her back, giving him full access, moaning as he took her nipple into his mouth. "Oh, God." She lowered herself, taking a little more of him, and then more, until he was deep inside, but he remained still, other than his tongue having a field day with her breast.

Pressing her hand against his chest, she sat up and reached between them, grinding wildly. While she knew she was in charge, she began to feel out of control. Not panicked, but desperate. She hadn't had an orgasm with a man inside her since right after she'd gotten married, before things went to hell.

She'd resented what Conrad had stolen from her, and she wanted to take it back.

Rubbing herself, she rocked back and forth. Her reckless need had taken over her thoughts. She could feel him swell inside, but out of nowhere, her body defined her, and she couldn't control the outcome.

She wouldn't be able to get herself there.

"Olympia," Landon said. "Don't make me use the safe word."

"What?" She stilled, staring at him. She clutched her breasts.

"Untie me, please," he said.

She lifted her knee off the bed.

"No," he said behind a tight jaw. "We're not done. You got what you needed when it came to one thing, now let me show you how you deserve to be loved."

* * *

Landon had no idea if he could please her or not, but he would die trying. And if not this time, he would try again.

And again.

Until he managed to permanently erase every bad thing that fucking asshole of a husband did to her.

He shook out the hand that had been freed. Surprisingly, he hadn't minded being tied up. The only reason why he wanted to stop was because he could tell this was no longer what she needed.

But he wasn't entirely sure of what was going to do it for her.

"I'm sorry," she whispered.

"For what? Because that was the best I've ever had." He cupped her cheeks and drew her in for a long kiss, doing his best to keep her still. He still needed a bit of a break if he was going to make this last long enough to show her anything.

"That's sweet," she said.

"It's the truth." He ran his hands down her back, letting his fingers dance across her spine. "Do you trust me?"

"I do."

He took a big risk and rolled her to her back, making sure to keep most of his weight on his hands. He held her gaze as he kissed the swell of her breast, rocking slowly against her body.

She flattened her hands on his chest as if to push him away, and he understood that need. He didn't need to be chest to chest. As a matter of fact, he enjoyed the slow pace while staring at her spirited eyes. He could see her soul inside the rich chocolate color. Everything about who she was came out in her eyes, and she held nothing back.

Not her fear.

And not her passion.

She bit down on her lower lip, and her breath came quicker.

He pulled out altogether.

"What are you doing?"

"Showing you how good it should be for you." He slipped his fingers inside her, curling them forward as she dropped her legs to the sides, thrusting her hips toward his hand. He lowered his head and kissed her hard nub. He flicked it with his tongue, making featherlike circles.

She tasted like honey and whiskey. He could easily get drunk on her, and his aching heart no longer hurt, but filled with a tickle of a bright new beginning.

She clenched his fingers with her insides with every roll of her hips, but this time there wasn't a sense of urgency that could never be fulfilled. But every time she came close, she stopped herself. It was as if she instantly froze right before she allowed herself to feel release.

He wondered if she didn't think she was worthy of the pleasure. If somehow that dick of a husband of hers stole that from her as well.

He kissed his way up her stomach, giving both breasts the attention they deserve, all while trying to put as little of his weight on her as possible. She'd said she wanted to be in control, but he suspected that had only been one aspect and now she needed to know how making love was a two-way street. A give and take. He needed to make her see she wasn't in this alone, and it wasn't all about him.

He kissed her nose, positioning his hands on either side of her shoulders. He arched his back slightly, entering her slowly. "Olympia, please open your eyes."

She blinked.

"I want to see you. Watch your face." He pushed

himself deep inside her before rocking back and plunging forward.

Biting her lip, her lashes fluttered.

"Stay with me," he whispered, gritting his teeth.

She was hot and sweet and kind and loving. She was everything a woman should be.

And more.

Her breathing turned rapid, and her fingernails dug into his pectoral muscles. Again, she didn't push him away, but she didn't pull him closer either. But she was on the edge, and this time he wasn't going to let her stop.

He reached between their bodies, and as he thrust, he found her clit with his index finger and flicked it back and forth, keeping their stares locked with one another.

She licked her lips, while her head jerked slightly left and right.

"That's it," he whispered. "Let go."

Without warning, she wrapped her arms and legs around his body, forcing him to collapse with his full weight on top of her. She took his mouth with a hot and wild kiss as her body bucked and thrashed about as her orgasm tore through her, rippling across her muscles and onto his.

His pulse pounded in his ears and he groaned,

letting his climax spill out while hers continued to grip his like a tight glove or a second skin.

He kissed the small space under her earlobe. "Are you okay?"

"I'm wonderful."

"Me too." He rolled to his side, pulling the covers over their bodies and snuggling in behind her. "We have one hour before I have to get up and shower. Can I hold you for until then?"

"As long as you don't snore in my ear."

"I can't promise I won't," he said. "I have a question for you."

"Okay. I'm all ears."

"How long did you rent the apartment next to mine?"

"It's a six-month lease." She turned her head. "Why?"

"After we find your brother, alive and well." He kissed her nose. "I'm guessing you'll want to stay and spend some time with him."

"That would be a good guess."

"Would there be room in that equation for dating a moody Navy SEAL who has commitment, trust, and a plethora of other issues, but has a case of the heavy likes for you?"

She laughed. "Heavy likes?"

"I've got it bad."

"You're cute." She patted his cheeks. "I think I might be able to make time, but only if we get to do that again."

"You won't have to twist my arm." He settled in behind her and closed his eyes. She held the power to break his heart.

But he didn't care.

In this moment, he knew his entire world had just been turned upside down.

His phone buzzed. "Shit," he groaned, reaching across her body.

"Do you have to answer it?"

"It's Tex," he said. "I'm putting it on speaker." He shifted to a sitting position. "Hey, Tex."

"Hey, man. I've got a lot to tell you."

"I'm all ears," Landon said. "So is Olympia."

"I've got good news and bad news. Which do you want first?"

"Just make it logical and fast." Landon watched as Olympia slipped from the bed, finding his shirt and slipping it over head. She sat at the end of the bed and brushed her hair.

Yeah. He had it real bad.

"I got into Woodrow's computer and found the source of the malware, and you're not going to like it."

Landon pinched the bridge of his nose. "Bring it."

"It's a software package written by the Navy and used by our government in anti-terrorism. I've seen it a hundred times. But this program was rewritten, something that would have to come down from higher ups, and I know it hasn't happened but maybe five times in ten years."

"But if someone thought Woodrow was a traitor, they would put that program on his machine, right?" Landon winced at the daggers coming from Olympia's eyes.

"To track him, sure. To read his emails, texts, find his location. But this was rewritten to include turning on the camera and audio without showing the green light. I was able to hook it up, rerouting it to Alaska, only to find out that all the intel coming off this machine is going right back to Little Creek."

"That's not earth-shattering," Landon admitted.

"Well, I was able to track it right down to the email it's being dumped to."

Landon bolted upright. "Now that has my attention."

"Quinn."

"No fucking way," Landon muttered, jumping from the bed, finding his fatigues. "She was just here.

We found plans that had gone missing when Woodrow went AWOL."

"Did you see those plans?" Tex asked.

"No. Quinn took them right quick." Landon hopped around his room, finding the rest of his uniform while Olympia rose to get dressed as well.

"I don't think they are the real plans," Tex said.

"But she'd figure that out the second she looked at them." Landon dropped his boot to the floor. "Fuck. That's by design."

"Is Olympia still in earshot?"

"I am," she said.

"There is a second malware software program installed in your brother's computer, and it was a little harder for me to find. As a matter of fact, I almost breezed right over it. But anyway, a history of the computer's activity is being sent to this email: *wondertwinspower@gmail.com*. Does that mean anything to you?"

"Oh, my God. Yes. When we were kids, we used to love to pretend we had superpowers."

"Is that his email?" Tex asked.

"Not that I know of, but I wouldn't put it past him to use something like that for a personal email," she said. "Should I reach out?"

"No," both Tex and Landon said at the same time.

"If he's been compromised or that email isn't what we think it is, it could put you in the in the line of fire," Tex said. "Let me look into it, and I'll be in touch."

"What about Commander Callahan? My brother didn't get along with him," she said.

"That's interesting, because Callahan doesn't like Quinn," Tex said.

"I didn't know that." Landon sat on the chair in the corner of his room and slipped on his boots. "Why and how did you find out?"

"I did some digging into Quinn's past and found out at her previous post she had a problem with a commanding officer."

"And that officer was Callahan." Landon let out a long breath. "I'm getting a headache. This seems like one big fucking complicated wild goose chase."

"It is, but I think it's also brilliant because if Quinn is our traitor, she can't really do anything because she needs a fall guy, and if Woodrow has been yanking her chain and sitting somewhere in a bunker playing his cards right, feeding us hints, leaving breadcrumbs, waiting to make a move, Quinn is fucked."

"But that note said they would kill my brother," Olympia said.

Landon took her by the hand and led her down the stairs. "That might be Quinn trying to find out if you had those plans. If what Tex is saying is true, Woodrow went to a lot of trouble to put fake plans in your safe, a key behind a toilet, and a million other little things to get us this far."

"And if we didn't get it right away, he'd be finding ways to send us messages because he's not in this alone," Tex said. "And this will blow your mind. Besides believing someone in the office has his back, I think Callahan does as well."

Landon snagged the keys to his Harley. He went to the front closet and pulled out the extra helmet, handing it to Olympia.

"But he always told me he has a problem with a high-ranking officer," Olympia said.

"Yeah, but Quinn is also up there in the ranks," Tex said. "And I'm starting to fall a little in love with this Woodrow fella. He's damn wicked smart, so I'm guessing he didn't want us getting too chummy with Callahan, so he planted that seed."

"And that gave Callahan some breathing room while we tried to snuggle up to Quinn." Landon shook his head. "We're heading to the base. Anything else we should know right now?"

"Nope," Tex said. "Just watch your back and keep Olympia in your sights."

"I will do both." He ended the call and stuffed his cell in his pocket. "I have a feeling this weekend you and I will be having your brother and Emily over for some steaks and a really expensive bottle of wine."

"I never thought I'd say this about being on a double date, but that sounds wonderful."

He curled his fingers around the front doorknob.

"Oh. Wait. My purse is upstairs." She turned on her heel just as he opened the door.

A sharp pain shot through the back of his head and rattled his teeth. He dropped to his knees.

"No! Landon!" Olympia took two steps toward him and skidded to a stop.

He reached out and touched the back of his skull and glanced at his bloody fingers. That wasn't good. Spots danced in front of his eyes as the room started to spin.

Another piercing jab tore through the side of his head. An echo filled his mind before everything went dark.

And silent.

CHAPTER 8

Olympia twisted and turned, struggling to break free from her restraints. She'd learned with her husband how to puff out her wrists so that she could wiggle out of things when Conrad was done. She wouldn't dream of defending herself because he would overpower her in a heartbeat, but it was for when he would leave her lying on the bathroom floor for hours, sometimes a full day. Panic gripped her heart, making it difficult to breathe. She had to free her hands. And she had to do it now, not after it was over.

She needed to break the way she handled her life, and it had to start right now.

Landon lay on the floor with his hands tied behind his back. At least he wasn't bleeding anymore, but he'd been out cold now for fifteen minutes, give or take. That couldn't be a good sign.

"Where's your fucking brother?" Quinn asked.

"I don't know," Olympia answered for the fifth time. She waggled and twisted her fingers. The rope wasn't overly tight, but Olympia had made a point to try to expand her muscles just so she could escape, something she was sure Quinn wouldn't think about.

"Look, we can do this the hard way or the easy way. It's up to you." Quinn waved her weapon in the air.

"I haven't a clue as to where he is. That's why I came here, to try to find him." Olympia slipped one finger through a loop in the rope. It was a start, if she didn't get stuck.

"Right. Then how the hell did you get fake top secret plans?"

"I wish I knew." When Olympia had been married to Conrad, stalling never did any good. Nor did lying. And telling the truth almost always landed her a fist in the face.

It was a damned if you do, damned if you don't.

This felt exactly the same way.

She shifted her gaze to Landon.

He winked.

Fuck. How long had he been awake?

She swallowed her breath. "I wish I could tell you where my brother is. I really do, because I don't do well being tied up." A second finger flipped through a section of the rope.

"I don't give a fuck."

Of course she didn't. Why would Quinn care, except maybe if Olympia freaked out, had a full-on panic attack, maybe that would give Landon enough time to miraculously loosen the ties that held his hands together.

Olympia shortened her breath. She'd had enough severe anxiety issues over the last few years; she should be able to fake this, though it wasn't that far off the mark considering her pulse increased to a dangerous level, and she could feel her heart slamming against her ribs.

"Now, this is the last time I'm going to ask nicely," Quinn said.

"I have a few guesses on where he might be."

"Are you kidding me?" Quinn stepped forward and raised her arm, backhanding Olympia across the face.

Olympia immediately tasted metal as the chair she was tied to wobbled, crashing to the floor, freeing her hands. She quickly made sure that she clasped her fingers together, holding the rope, making sure it didn't fall.

Quinn bent over and yanked her back upright.

Landon moaned.

"Look who is waking up." Quinn turned her back to Olympia and kicked Landon in the gut.

"Jesus," Landon muttered. "Was that really necessary?"

"Tell me where Woodrow is, and I can promise I won't do it again." Quinn stepped over him, shoving her gun into his chest. "That said, I will guarantee you no matter what, you're a dead man."

"Really? And how are you going to get away with that?"

"Oh, that's simple," Quinn said. "You see, you really shouldn't sleep with the enemy."

"Well, then, thank God I'm not sleeping with you," he said.

She pressed the gun against his temple.

Olympia bit back a scream. Needing to fake a panic attack was no longer necessary.

"Don't fuck with me," Quinn said. "I'm not in the mood for games. So, this is how it will go down, whether I get what I need or not. Your new fuck buddy will kill you, and I'm going to come in and kill her, after figuring out she was in cahoots with her brother."

"What's the evidence against me?" Olympia asked, desperate to get the gun out of Landon's face.

"Those stupid fake files your brother put in your safe to throw me off the trail. But it didn't work. Now, if you would just tell me where he is, I might make this easier for you."

"Easier how?" Landon asked.

"Well, for starters, both of you will die quick and painless. And secondly, Landon, I won't make you watch her die a slow and tortuous death. I know how that is such a hot button knowing your son didn't die right away, that he lingered on for hours after your wife—"

"Shut the fuck up," Olympia said. She needed to draw Quinn's attention back toward her. If she could get her close enough, maybe, just maybe, she could knock the gun out of her hands.

"You're going to tell me what to do?" Quinn asked. "That's rich."

"I am. Because if you want to know where my brother is, you're going to have to do one thing."

"What's that?" Quinn inched closer, but she pointed the gun toward the ground.

"I don't have a fucking clue." Olympia cocked her fist and took a quick jab at Quinn's nose.

Quinn dropped her weapon, clutching her face and stumbling backward.

As fast as she could, Olympia snagged the weapon.

"Untie me," Landon commanded.

Quinn took a step forward.

Olympia raised the gun and shot at the ceiling. "You must not know that I killed my husband in self-defense." She lowered the gun, pointing it at Quinn's chest. "I won't shoot to kill, but I will shoot to maim."

Quinn raised her hands and moved toward the front of the house.

"And that right there is the woman I think I'm falling madly in love with," Landon said. "Now, please, untie me."

Quinn turned and reached for the door, but someone pushed it open.

"I don't think you're going anywhere." A military cop stepped through the door.

Olympia raced to Landon's side and quickly untied his hands. "This is becoming a thing with us."

"Don't get used to it," Landon said, taking her

into his arms. "It was fun once, but I don't think I want to be tied up by anyone again. Not even you."

She wrapped her arms around him and let out a long breath. "I'm okay with that," she murmured. "Do you think it will be hard to find my brother now?"

"Nope," the sound of her twin's voice filled the room.

"Woodrow?" She glanced toward the door. "Is that you?"

"In the flesh." Woodrow waltzed into the apartment sporting a smile as if nothing happened. And right behind him was Emily.

The military police escorted Quinn out the door in handcuffs.

"You fucking asshole." Olympia made a beeline for her brother and poked him dead center in the chest. "How could you fuck with me like that?"

"I think Landon over there has the right to be more pissed off," Woodrow said, taking her into his arms and giving her a big hug.

Landon stood, shaking out his hands. "I'll get over it as long as you're buying a big-ass steak dinner tonight. Actually, every night this week."

"That can be arranged." Woodrow stretched out his hand.

Landon pushed it aside and gave Woodrow a good man hug. "You were right. Your sister does like me, and I think we'll be spending a lot of time together."

Woodrow smiled. "See, sis. I do know how to pick 'em."

CHAPTER 9

Five months later...

Landon poked the steaks. Flames flickered from the grill. Smoke billowed into the air, sending the smell of sizzling beef cooking over an open flame into his nostrils.

But that didn't take care of Landon's heartburn.

Or his perpetual increased pulse.

Or his constant nerves.

"You're quiet tonight." Woodrow slapped him on the back before handing him a beer.

"Just tired. Even though the deployment was only a week, it was brutal," Landon said. But the reality was being away from Olympia was the most difficult part, but they had discussed his career a million times, and it was important to both of them that he remain a SEAL.

He agreed. Giving it up right now would be a mistake, even though he'd do it in heartbeat, if she asked. But he struggled with a plan on what he'd do outside of the military.

She knew she could have a career anywhere. No matter where in the world the military took him, she could always have her life as it was now.

That was if she chose to follow him.

Though the likelihood he'd be stationed anywhere outside of Virginia in the near future was slim to none.

With her lease being up in a month, they had some decisions to make, and both of them had been avoiding the conversation.

"Emily and I didn't have to come over tonight," Woodrow said.

"No. It's fine. Besides, I know Olympia has been looking forward to it."

"But you two need some alone time as well."

"Olympia wanted to plan out Emily's bridal shower and all that. She's really excited about the two of you getting married. It's all she talks about."

"Not with me," Woodrow said. "All I ever hear about is you. It's cringeworthy."

Landon laughed. But his nerves cut it short.

"What's wrong?" Woodrow asked.

"Nothing."

"Bullshit."

In the last few months, Landon had gotten to know Woodrow on a different level, and they had become more than friends.

"We haven't talked much about what happens when her lease is up, and I don't want her to leave."

"I've got it on good authority that she doesn't want move either." Woodrow squeezed his shoulder. "I know what my sister has been through, and I have an idea of what you've experienced, and neither narrative is pretty. I understand that while you love each other, your relationship hasn't been simple. You both have a shit ton of baggage. That said, I know Olympia, and she needs you to ask her to stay."

"I know that," Landon said. "But will this be over the top." He pulled the engagement ring out of his pocket. "Because it's a little much for me, and my heart is racing, and my palms are sweating, but I don't ever want to know what life would be like without her in it."

"I knew when I picked you to protect my sister

that you'd not only step up and do it, but that you'd do it forever." Woodrow took the grilling fork out of Landon's hands. "I'll take care of dinner. You go make sure my sister makes the right decision."

Landon didn't hesitate. He strolled across the back patio until he stood in front of the girls. "Excuse me. Mind if I have a moment alone with Olympia?"

"Not at all." Emily took the hint and made a beeline for Woodrow.

"Hello there, handsome." Olympia raised up on tiptoe and kissed him full-out on the lips. "I know you're exhausted and would rather just spend a day or two in bed in front of the television, so I really appreciate this one night with Woodrow and Emily."

"No. This is fine. I really enjoy being around family. And it's only a few hours. Besides, you'll let me sleep in tomorrow."

"Of course I will."

"Or maybe you won't," he said with an arched brow.

She cocked her head. "What does that mean?"

"I love you."

"I love you back," she said with pursed lips. "Whenever you get like this, it's because you are about to be deployed or you're about to pick a fight over something stupid."

"I can promise you this is neither."

"Okay. I'm intrigued."

There was no reason to be totally traditional. She wouldn't want him to get on one knee and be all weird and romantic. She'd want him to be pragmatic and logical.

"Your lease is up next month."

"I know," she said.

"I'd love it if you'd move in here with me."

She arched a brow. "Are you formally asking me?"

"Yes," he said.

"Thank God. I thought I was going to have to just start sneaking my stuff in here and wonder if you'd notice I became your roommate."

He chuckled but quickly turned somber. "There's more."

"Excuse me?"

He held up the ring. "I want it to be permanent, forever, and official. I want us to be married," he said. "And for the record, I don't expect you to take my last name. I know how you feel about that."

She took the ring and slipped it onto her ring finger.

It was a perfect fit.

"I don't know. Asher is a good, solid, strong name."

He opened his mouth, but no words came out.

"I hope you don't want a big wedding or anything. I'm kind of down for getting married at the chapel on base as soon as possible."

This was going so much better than he expected. "I'm absolutely fine with that. But I don't want to take away from your brother and Emily."

Olympia leaned in. "We already have," she whispered, taking his hand and pressing it against her stomach.

"What? I'm not following you."

"I'm a couple of weeks late, and while you were gone, I took a pregnancy test, and it turns out, we're expecting."

"We're fucking what?" He gripped her hips for support. "How did that happen?"

"Well, it started with us having sex and birth control failing."

He blinked. "It was rhetorical," he mumbled. "A baby."

"Are you okay?" she asked.

"I think so," he said. "Are you sure?"

"We both know we still have a lot to work

through; its why we see a therapist, but yeah, I'm good. And I'm happy. I want this child. And I want a life with you."

He cupped her cheeks. "I've never been happier. I love you so much it hurts, and I can't wait to meet out baby." He rested his hand on her belly. "But we might need to find a bigger place."

"Wyatt and Clover said there is a house near theirs for sale."

Landon lowered his chin. "Do they know we're having a kid?"

Olympia shook her head. "But I did tell them I wanted to stay and if you didn't bring up marriage, I was going to."

"How did I get so lucky?" he asked.

"I think we have my brother to thank for that."

Thank you for taking the time to read *Protecting Olympia.* Please feel free to leave an HONEST review on Amazon, Goodreads, and Bookbub!

Sign up for my Newsletter (https://dl.bookfunnel.com/

6atcf7g1be) where I often give away free books before publication.

Join my private Facebook group (https://www.facebook.com/groups/191706547909047/) where I post exclusive excerpts and discuss all things murder and love!

Never miss a new release. Follow me on Amazon:amazon.com/author/jentalty

And on Bookbub: bookbub.com/authors/jentalty

ABOUT THE AUTHOR

Welcome to my World! I'm a USA Today Bestseller of Romantic Suspense, Contemporary Romance, and Paranormal Romance.

I first started writing while carting my kids to one hockey rink after the other, averaging 170 games per year between 3 kids in 2 countries and 5 states. My first book, IN TWO WEEKS was originally published in 2007. In 2010 I helped form a publishing company (Cool Gus Publishing) with NY Times Bestselling Author Bob Mayer where I ran the technical side of the business through 2016.

I'm currently enjoying the next phase of my life...the empty NESTER! My husband and I spend our winters in Jupiter, Florida and our summers in Rochester, NY. We have three amazing children who have all gone off to carve out their places in the world, while I continue to craft stories that I hope will make you readers feel good and put a smile on your face.

Sign up for my Newsletter (https://dl.bookfunnel.com/6atcf7g1be) where I often give away free books before publication.

Join my private Facebook group (https://www.facebook.com/groups/191706547909047/) where I post exclusive excerpts and discuss all things murder and love!

Never miss a new release. Follow me on Amazon:amazon.com/author/jentalty

And on Bookbub: bookbub.com/authors/jen-talty

ALSO BY JEN TALTY

BRAND NEW SERIES!

The Monroes

COLOR ME YOURS

COLOR ME SMART

It's all in the Whiskey

JOHNNIE WALKER

GEORGIA MOON

JACK DANIELS

JIM BEAM

Search and Rescue

PROTECTING AINSLEY

PROTECTING CLOVER

PROTECTING OLYMPIA

NY State Trooper Series

IN TWO WEEKS

DARK WATER

DEADLY SECRETS

MURDER IN PARADISE BAY

TO PROTECT HIS OWN

DEADLY SEDUCTION

WHEN A STRANGER CALLS

NY State Trooper Novella

HIS DEADLY PAST

Brand New Novella for the First Responders series

A spin off from the NY State Troopers series

PLAYING WITH FIRE

PRIVATE CONVERSATION

The Men of Thief Lake

REKINDLED

DESTINY'S DREAM

Federal Investigators

JANE DOE'S RETURN

THE BUTTERFLY MURDERS

The Aegis Network

THE LIGHTHOUSE

HER LAST HOPE

THE LAST FLIGHT

THE RETURN HOME

THE MATRIARCH

The Collective Order

THE LOST SISTER

THE LOST SOLDIER

THE LOST SOUL

Coming soon!

THE LOST CONNECTION

Special Forces Operation Alpha

BURNING DESIRE

BURNING KISS

BURNING SKIES

BURNING LIES

BURNING HEART

BURNING BED

REMEMBER ME ALWAYS

The Brotherhood Protectors

Out of the Wild

ROUGH JUSTICE

ROUGH AROUND THE EDGES

ROUGH RIDE

ROUGH EDGE

ROUGH BEAUTY

The Brotherhood Protectors

The Saving Series

SAVING LOVE

Holiday Romances

A Christmas Getaway

Alaskan Christmas

WHISPERS

Heroes & Heroines on the Field

Taking A Risk

Tee Time

The Twilight Crossing Series

THE BLIND DATE

SPRING FLING

SUMMER'S GONE

WINTER WEDDING

Witches and Werewolves

LADY SASS

ALL THAT SASS

Coming soon!

NEON SASS

PAINTING SASS

Boxsets

LOVE CHRISTMAS, MOVIES

UNFORGETABLE PASSION

UNFORGETABLE CHARMERS

A NIGHT SHE'LL REMEMBER

SWEET AND SASSY IN THE SNOW

SWEET AND SASSY PRINCE CHARMING

PROTECT AND DESIRE

SWEET AND SASSY BABY LOVE

CHRISTMAS AT MISTLETOE LODGE

THE PLAYERS: OVERCOMING THE ODDS

CHRISTMAS SHORTS

CHRISTMAS DREAMS

All That Glitters

INVINCIBLE SECRETS

UNFORGETABLE SUSPENSE

Nov*ellas*

NIGHTSHADE

There are many more books in this fan fiction world than listed here, for an up-to-date list go to www.AcesPress.com

You can also visit our Amazon page at: http://www.amazon.com/author/operationalpha

Special Forces: Operation Alpha World

Christie Adams: Charity's Heart
Denise Agnew: Dangerous to Hold
Shauna Allen: Awakening Aubrey
Brynne Asher: Blackburn
Linzi Baxter: Unlocking Dreams
Jennifer Becker: Hiding Catherine
Alice Bello: Shadowing Milly
Heather Blair: Rescue Me
Anna Blakely: Rescuing Gracelynn
Amy Briggs: Saving Sarah
Julia Bright: Saving Lorelei
Victoria Bright: Surviving Savage
Cara Carnes: Protecting Mari
Kendra Mei Chailyn: Beast
Melissa Kay Clarke: Rescuing Annabeth
Samantha A. Cole: Handling Haven
Sue Coletta: Hacked
Melissa Combs: Gallant

Anne Conley: Redemption for Misty
KaLyn Cooper: Rescuing Melina
Liz Crowe: Marking Mariah
Sarah Curtis: Securing the Odds
Jordan Dane: Redemption for Avery
Tarina Deaton: Found in the Lost
Aspen Drake, Intense
KL Donn: Unraveling Love
Riley Edwards: Protecting Olivia
PJ Fiala: Defending Sophie
Nicole Flockton: Protecting Maria
Michele Gwynn: Rescuing Emma
Casey Hagen: Shielding Nebraska
Desiree Holt: Protecting Maddie
Kathy Ivan: Saving Sarah
Kris Jacen, Be With Me
Jesse Jacobson: Protecting Honor
Silver James: Rescue Moon
Becca Jameson: Saving Sofia
Kate Kinsley: Protecting Ava
Heather Long: Securing Arizona
Gennita Low: No Protection
Kirsten Lynn: Joining Forces for Jesse
Margaret Madigan: Bang for the Buck
Kimberly McGath: The Predecessor
Rachel McNeely: The SEAL's Surprise Baby

KD Michaels: Saving Laura
Lynn Michaels, Rescuing Kyle
Wren Michaels: The Fox & The Hound
Kat Mizera: Protecting Bobbi
Keira Montclair, Wolf and the Wild Scots
Mary B Moore: Force Protection
LeTeisha Newton: Protecting Butterfly
Angela Nicole: Protecting the Donna
MJ Nightingale: Protecting Beauty
Sarah O'Rourke: Saving Liberty
Victoria Paige: Reclaiming Izabel
Anne L. Parks: Mason
Debra Parmley: Protecting Pippa
Lainey Reese: Protecting New York
TL Reeve and Michele Ryan: Extracting Mateo
Elena M. Reyes: Keeping Ava
Angela Rush: Charlotte
Rose Smith: Saving Satin
Jenika Snow: Protecting Lily
Lynne St. James: SEAL's Spitfire
Dee Stewart: Conner
Harley Stone: Rescuing Mercy
Jen Talty: Burning Desire
Reina Torres, Rescuing Hi'ilani
Megan Vernon: Protecting Us

Police and Fire: Operation Alpha World

Freya Barker: Burning for Autumn

Julia Bright, Justice for Amber

Anna Brooks, Guarding Georgia

KaLyn Cooper: Justice for Gwen

Aspen Drake: Sheltering Emma

Deanndra Hall: Shelter for Sharla

Barb Han: Kace

EM Hayes: Gambling for Ashleigh

CM Steele: Guarding Hope

Reina Torres: Justice for Sloane

Aubree Valentine, Justice for Danielle

Stacey Wilk: Stage Fright

Tarpley VFD Series

Silver James, Fighting for Elena

Deanndra Hall, Fighting for Carly

Haven Rose, Fighting for Calliope

MJ Nightingale, Fighting for Jemma

TL Reeve, Fighting for Brittney

Nicole Flockton, Fighting for Nadia

As you know, this book included at least one character from Susan Stoker's books. To check out more, see below.

SEAL of Protection: Legacy Series

Securing Caite

Securing Brenae (novella)

Securing Sidney

Securing Piper

Securing Zoey

Securing Avery (May 2020)

Securing Kalee (Sept 2020)

Securing Jane (novella) (Feb 2021)

SEAL Team Hawaii Series

Finding Elodie (Apr 2021)

Finding Lexie (Aug 2021)

Finding Kenna (Oct 2021)

Finding Monica (TBA)

Finding Carly (TBA)

Finding Ashlyn (TBA)

Delta Team Two Series

Shielding Gillian

Shielding Kinley (Aug 2020)

Shielding Aspen (Oct 2020)

Shielding Riley (Jan 2021)

Shielding Devyn (May 2021)

Shielding Ember (Sep 2021)

Shielding Sierra (TBA)

Delta Force Heroes Series

Rescuing Rayne (FREE!)

Rescuing Aimee (novella)

Rescuing Emily

Rescuing Harley

Marrying Emily (novella)

Rescuing Kassie

Rescuing Bryn

Rescuing Casey

Rescuing Sadie (novella)

Rescuing Wendy

Rescuing Mary

Rescuing Macie (Novella)

Badge of Honor: Texas Heroes Series

Justice for Mackenzie (FREE!)

Justice for Mickie

Justice for Corrie

Justice for Laine (novella)

Shelter for Elizabeth

Justice for Boone
Shelter for Adeline
Shelter for Sophie
Justice for Erin
Justice for Milena
Shelter for Blythe
Justice for Hope
Shelter for Quinn
Shelter for Koren
Shelter for Penelope

SEAL of Protection Series

Protecting Caroline (FREE!)
Protecting Alabama
Protecting Fiona
Marrying Caroline (novella)
Protecting Summer
Protecting Cheyenne
Protecting Jessyka
Protecting Julie (novella)
Protecting Melody
Protecting the Future
Protecting Kiera (novella)
Protecting Alabama's Kids (novella)
Protecting Dakota

New York Times, USA Today and *Wall Street Journal* Bestselling Author Susan Stoker has a heart as big as the state of Tennessee where she lives, but this all American girl has also spent the last fourteen years living in Missouri, California, Colorado, Indiana, and Texas. She's married to a retired Army man who now gets to follow *her* around the country.

www.stokeraces.com
www.AcesPress.com
susan@stokeraces.com

Made in the USA
Monee, IL
18 May 2020

31381660R00105